The Light Across the River

The Light Across the River

A Novel

Stephanie Reed

Kregel Publications

To my friends, with love

Acknowledgments

For their help, the author is grateful to
- Writer and poet Donna E., and fellow Kregel author Susan K. Marlow, for their faithful reading of many drafts and their constant encouragement
- Shane, a direct descendant of Johnny Rankin and Mary Ann Hay, and his family, for permission to tell his ancestor's story
- Christian herbalist Sarah Brown, for information about the herbs Eliza used
- Nancy Saul, for her hospitality, and for information about the Reverend Mahan
- The staff at the Ohio Historical Society, for their location of the Rankin family papers
- The wonderful people at Kregel Publications
- Photographer Jill Clark and Noah M., for their portrayal of Johnny
- All my friends and family who prayed for me and encouraged me as I wrote this book, especially Clara, Dan, Donna E., Donna S., Ev, Hannah, Jill, Laura, Maria, Paula, Steve, Susan, Ted, Tom, and Walter
- The One who enabled me to tell this story, my Lord and Savior Jesus Christ

Part 1
1837–1838

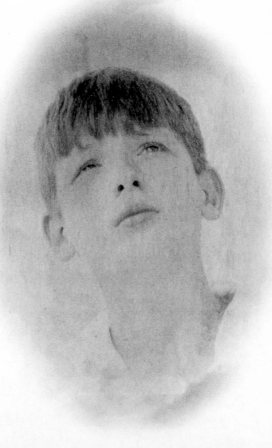

Chapter 1

JOHNNY

JOHNNY RANKIN HID FROM his dozen siblings up in a hedge apple tree that stood on the hill behind Ripley. Wrinkling his nose at the spicy scent of October, he shifted his feet on the sturdy branch, leaned against the trunk, and daydreamed. His hat brim shaded his eyes from the late-afternoon glints from the distant Ohio River.

Slam!

Johnny squinted through the yellow leaves toward the back door of his house. So much for solitude—his eldest brother, Lowry, and their neighbor, Miss Amanda Kephart, now stood in the back yard, talking with their heads close together.

My, Mandy's pretty.

Johnny had first seen her in the church choir when he was six. Right then and there, he'd made up his mind to marry her. That was five years ago; he hoped she could wait another seven years until he was old enough. Meanwhile, maybe he'd sneak off and pick another bunch of wildflowers to leave on her doorstep.

Too late! Lowry and Mandy were strolling toward his hiding place. He could barely make out what they were saying.

"Please may I tell, Lowry?" Mandy's sunbonnet hid her face.

"Not until everything's settled." Lowry sounded like Father. Trust a preacher to be rock-solid sure. Johnny rubbed his itchy nose and wondered what her secret could be.

"I wish I could have told my father. Sometimes I can't believe . . . cholera!" Mandy bowed her head. "So quick." Johnny's heart ached for her.

"I know," he heard his brother say. Lowry glanced toward the house before he took Mandy's hand. Then he led her behind the close-grown row of hedge apple trees to a spot just below where Johnny was perched, though he couldn't see them.

Lowry was holding Mandy's hand.

He heard the rustle of fabric.

She must have sat down.

With Lowry.

Johnny dug his fingernails into his upper lip. *Was Lowry still holding her hand?* He peeked, but all he could see was the crown of his brother's hat. He gritted his teeth and kept still.

He cast about for a diversion and saw a gray squirrel on a branch above his head, going after a bumpy hedge apple. Squirrels craved hedge apple seeds. Getting to them was difficult, but this squirrel seemed determined. The fruit would have to ripen before the feast began, but what was time to a squirrel?

A corner of Johnny's mouth lifted. Good thing the squirrel didn't care how foolish it looked. It hooked its hindmost toes around a twig and pushed until the hedge apple turned. Patient paws scrabbled. Now the hedge apple dangled by a sliver of bark. One more tap, and it plummeted—right toward Lowry's hat.

Johnny snagged it in the nick of time. The disgusted squirrel whisked to another tree while Johnny wedged the green globe into a notch between two branches. He wrinkled his nose again and sniffed at the pungent sap on his fingers. Whew! His eyes watered. He shut them. His mouth opened. Closed. Opened again. Then he reared back and sneezed. The sound of it ricocheted over the rooftops of Ripley.

When Johnny opened his eyes, Lowry was staring up at him. "Why, you sneaky little spy!" He made a grab for Johnny's leg.

Thorns snagged Johnny's trousers as he scrambled upward, out of reach. He clambered along the hedge apple limb until it bent and whipped him to a flying start ahead of Lowry. Just a few more strides and he would beat his older brother to the steep place and escape down the steps to town.

The next thing he knew, he was pitching forward. The hillside came up at him faster than he could run. His arms and legs windmilled. He grabbed something—a weed—but the dry leaves stripped away under his fingers. An empty feeling shot through his middle, like he'd left his stomach behind. Then a stone bounced down the hill, and so did Johnny.

He already knew two ways to travel the half mile to town, but now he discovered a new one. He somersaulted over weeds, skidded on loose clay, and cartwheeled through dry blackberry canes. His hat flew off, and he thought his teeth would shake loose.

By the time he rolled into Ripley, his head orbited his body, or at least it felt that way. He moaned and clutched his temples to hold the world still.

"Johnny, are you hurt?" Mandy sounded far away.

Boots scrunched on gravel. "Serves him right," Lowry puffed. Shadows loomed. Johnny felt Lowry's rough grip. Mandy supported his elbow, and they helped him to his feet. "Let this be a lesson to you." Lowry whacked the dust out of Johnny's hat and jammed it back on his head. "Stop spying on everybody and mind your own business."

Mandy cleared her throat and Lowry grew less gruff. "Anything broken?"

"No," Johnny croaked. His head ached too much to shake, and his ears were ringing.

"Well, come on, then."

Every step hurt as they climbed the big hill. When they reached the summit, the Rankins' dinner bell stopped midclang.

"Johnny!" The bell rope snaked out of Mother's hands. "What in this world?" She slapped dust and picked burrs from his clothes. "See that you get this mess cleaned off before you come to supper. Mandy, will you help him, please?" Mother bustled away with Lowry at her heels.

Why doesn't Mother just say I'm a naughty little boy and be done with it? His shoulders drooped as he followed Mandy to the back porch.

"It's a miracle you're not bad hurt," she said. "Such a tumble! See, your trousers are ripped here . . . and here." She tilted his chin; her touch burned. "Your cheek's scratched, too."

He shrugged and hung his head. Mandy filled the washbasin with fresh water and moistened her handkerchief. With one hand on Johnny's shoulder, she dabbed his cuts and scratches clean. He hardly noticed how the soap stung; he was too busy brooding about how no one in his family cared much what happened to him. Thirteen children divided by one mother and father left no time for mollycoddling.

Twilight had fallen by the time Johnny took his seat at the long harvest table. Supper smelled heavenly. His mouth watered while Father said grace and passed the plates to the seven girls along the opposite side of the table. At the far end, Mother struggled to keep baby Tappan's hands away from the hot serving bowls. Finally, supper traveled along the line to the four boys to his right, then to Johnny. He helped himself to a golden heap of sweet corn and all the mashed potatoes his plate could hold before he passed the bowls to William and Andrew. Lowry glowered at the amount on Johnny's plate, but no one else did. Sometimes it was good to be the shortest, skinniest boy in the family.

Hunger kept anyone from commenting on Johnny's appearance. Sam bolted his meal like a colicky horse, sighed, stretched, and patted his stomach. "What's going on in town,

Cal? Somebody been fighting?" He raised an eyebrow at Johnny, who ignored him.

"Not that I've heard," Cal snorted. "Nothing ever happens in Ripley."

"Now, Cal." Mother waggled a finger. "That's the way we want it. Remember, you and Sam are on duty tonight."

"All right, Mother. May I have the biscuits, please?"

Father passed the bowl. "You two will do well if nothing happens," he said. "Laban Biggerman has sought an opportunity to best us since James's slave, Paul, escaped last month." He shook his head. "Reverend Mahan ought not to have kept him around so long."

"Well, it wasn't for lack of warning," Lowry chimed in. "The last thing I told the Reverend was to keep the fugitive ahead of the pursuers, just before Alex and I left for the music convention at Sardinia." He handed the bowl to David, who passed it to Cal.

Oh, yes, Lowry was always right. Johnny wanted to roll his eyes. As he held out his hand for the biscuits, Johnny saw a secret smile flash between Lowry and Mandy. She blushed pink and inspected her plate.

Johnny chomped his sweet corn. The very idea of Lowry looking at Mandy that way rankled him. Lowry had accused him of spying, too—said he did it all the time. As if Johnny were at fault when people stumbled across his best hiding places. Worst by far, Lowry had held Mandy's hand.

The words flashed out quicker than thought. "I know what's happening in Ripley. Mandy knows something that Lowry won't let her tell." He shot a triumphant glance at Lowry.

"How do you know, Johnny?" Father used his Sunday voice, the one that you could hear from any place in the sanctuary.

Johnny knew how to hold his tongue . . . sometimes. He traced a knothole in the chestnut plank that Lowry had hand-finished.

Sure enough, Lowry butted in. "How does he know? Why, everyone in Ripley says if you want to hear the news, go ask Johnny."

"That's not true!"

"Oh, no?" Lowry addressed Father again. "What would you say about a boy who listens to a private conversation and then repeats it? He was in the hedge apple tree spying while Mandy and I watched the sun set."

"I wasn't either spying!" Johnny said. "I just wanted to be by myself. And I was, until you came along holding Mandy's hand."

Mother's knife clattered. "Why, Lowry!"

Lowry withered Johnny with a glance. "That proves it. You can't hold your tongue. I wouldn't be surprised to hear that you've let slip about the Underground."

Johnny clenched his fists, but Father held up a hand.

"Boys, that's enough. But, Lowry"—Father's lips thinned—"do I understand you and Amanda wished to be alone? Holding hands?"

The whole table waited to hear what Lowry would say. Johnny gloated until he saw Mandy blush. Her distress rubbed the gloss right off his big revelation.

"Father, I would never . . . that is, Miss Kephart and I . . ." Lowry spluttered.

"My, how formal, Lowry! It seems we've waited long enough to share this . . ." Mandy's eyes sparkled with tears. "On the way home from Sardinia, Lowry asked me to marry him, and I've accepted." She appealed to Father and Mother. "May we have your blessing?"

Benches and chairs scraped as a throng of Rankins converged on the pair. Father shook Lowry's hand; Mother hugged Mandy. They laughed and cried at the same time. The girls squealed, "Why didn't you tell us?" The boys thumped Lowry's back.

Johnny lost count of how many times he heard, "God bless you!" Joy filled the room, and for once even grouchy old Lowry grinned.

No one saw Johnny slip out the door.

He climbed the hedge apple tree and hunched alone in the chilly darkness. When would things ever change? Brothers and sisters crammed in edgewise, all of them taller, stronger, faster, or smarter than he was. Father and Mother frantically busy with the church, family, and a million other things. They never took any more notice of him than to say, "Johnny, do this," or "Johnny, do that."

The only person who'd ever paid him any mind was Mandy, and now she belonged to Lowry. That hurt, but what surprised him more was how much Lowry's words hurt. He'd as good as called Johnny a traitor by implying that he would spill the family secret.

He could not deny that it was tempting to tell about the Underground. The older boys and Ibby told exciting stories about how the family helped fugitive slaves. What frustrated the life out of him was that he must never breathe a word to anyone else. Why couldn't Father see how wrong it was to keep quiet? It seemed so simple to Johnny. If only people could know how horrible slavery was! If only they knew the great risks men took to be free!

A flicker caught his eye; somebody had placed the signal light in the upstairs window. The soft glow steadied. Further back than Johnny remembered, lights had burned in the two side windows and in the front. When a slave across the river in Kentucky wanted to know where John Rankin lived, he looked for the light.

The yard brightened and dimmed. Somebody had come out the front door. Sure enough, two dark shapes swished through the wet grass toward the hill; Cal and Sam were headed to town.

They would pass the evening at Thomas McCague's house on Front Street to watch for fugitive slaves. Father still refused to go to Kentucky to help the slaves, but whenever possible, he offered aid the minute they set foot on Ohio soil. So long as slave escapes continued thicker than raisins in a pie, that would remain the rule.

Johnny knew Father's other rules, too: keep the fugitive ahead of the pursuers, use a different station each time, and never talk to anyone—not even his best friends—about the runaways. But had Father ever let him be a conductor? No, and he was older than Lowry had been when he first conducted.

Lowry's remark still burned. Perhaps if Johnny assured Father that he would never reveal the family business, he would make him a conductor.

He vaulted from the tree, bound and determined. Tomorrow night he would keep watch from Thomas McCague's house.

Chapter 2

ELIZA

ELIZA SNAPPED HER DUST rag out the front door and plodded to the sideboard. A multitude of dusty gimcracks cluttered its surface, but that suited her just fine. She picked up the china dog and rubbed it, then dusted under it. She moved mighty slow and quiet because it was Bible reading time. What would she hear today?

"I love you, Mama."

"I love you, too, darlin'." Missus James stroked Viola's hair and kissed Pansy. The three sat on the striped davenport in the parlor, their backs to Eliza. The daughters rested their heads on Missus James's shoulders as she read aloud to them. "'Charity suffereth long, and is kind; charity envieth not; charity vaunteth not itself, is not puffed up . . .'"

"Mama, what's charity?"

"Charity is love. . . . 'Doth not behave itself unseemly, seeketh not her own, is not easily provoked, thinketh no evil; rejoiceth not in iniquity, but rejoiceth in the truth; beareth all things, believeth all things, hopeth all things, endureth all things. Charity never faileth.'" Missus James closed the Bible. "Now, who can show me charity?" Pansy and Viola hugged their mama hard. "You're going to squeeze me in two!" she protested with a smile.

Eliza polished the sideboard with resentful strokes. *Now ain't that fine, for Missus James to love on her children anytime*

she pleases? Hard to see when Eliza could find such time with
her own children, Beulah and baby Mose. She pursed her lips
and flicked the rag at a slender bud vase. It teetered and crashed
to the floor.

"Oh, what a pity, Eliza. No, don't trouble your head about that
old thing. Just see to it that you get all the glass up, so my girls
don't run a sliver in their feet. By the way, Mr. Biggerman will
be joining us for supper, so set an extra place." Missus James
turned away. "Now, darlings, I will hear your music."

The piano skittered from note to note like a kitten was on the
keys. Eliza fished the shards of glass from the rug and walked
stiffly to the kitchen. She worked up biscuit dough and slapped
it out on the floury board while she fumed.

Here she was, making supper for the likes of Laban Biggerman. It was hard to think up a worse chore. The overseer called
Eliza "Ol' Ugly," but she could stand that. He looked at her
grown daughter, Beulah, like a white man had no business to
look at a young woman raising five children on her own. That
was harder to bear, but Eliza kept a close eye on Biggerman.
Beulah's family lived in Eliza's cabin because there was more
safety in numbers.

The way Biggerman looked at Eliza's husband, George, now,
that was what wore Eliza to a frazzle. She tried to put it out of
her mind as she fixed supper, but—lawsy mercy! She knocked
over the cut glass saltcellar. The salt flew one way and the square
silver salt spoon with the pea pod etched in the handle flew the
other. Eliza groaned to her knees and fetched the spoon. She
swept the salt up, threw a pinch over her left shoulder, stood the
broom in its corner, and refilled the saltcellar.

Goodness gracious, this kitchen is hot! Eliza flapped her apron
and glanced idly out the window toward her cabin, like she did
a hundred times a day. Grapevines swarmed up the logs on one
side. She could smell her herb garden from here, mingled scents

of sage, mint, and yarrow. Dead pea vines and beanstalks rattled when the wind blew.

In the midst of it all stood George. He fooled around the dooryard with a happy smile on his face. There wasn't much Eliza could trust him to do, but she'd scattered some dried bean and pea pods on the ground this morning so he could walk in a circle and trample them. That was how George threshed. Later, the children would gather the shelled peas and beans.

The sight of George's faithful treading warmed Eliza's heart, but the next instant it nearly stopped beating. Laban Biggerman was hiding behind the currant bushes near her cabin. He was watching George, too.

A coldness crawled clean through Eliza's body. The overseer's hands were empty, but she knew he meant business. He clenched and unclenched his fists like he was choking the life out of George. Eliza clutched at her throat.

Then Biggerman turned his dead eyes to Eliza, like he knew she was watching. His mustache gleamed like a new copper kettle in the late afternoon sun. He flicked the brim of his slouch hat in a mock salute and walked away.

❧

The thought of Biggerman's lifeless eyes troubled her all evening, even while George cracked jokes and cut a shine. Here in their cabin it was easy to pretend that nothing was wrong. There were Beulah's children and baby Mose to care for, a second supper to cook, and evening chores to keep her mind occupied, but it was time she faced up to facts. She could not watch out for George the livelong day. His life was in danger here.

She'd kept him safe for so long. Mr. James flew off the handle when he got angry at George and his foolish ways, but Eliza and

Missus James kept him simmered down. The day Biggerman came—that was when the real trouble began.

Strong though George was, Biggerman quickly discovered he was too addled to be of much use. The overseer often raged at George, but George only grinned. Missus James warned Biggerman that George must not be touched because he was a "poor unfortunate." At first, Eliza had been thankful, but now she wondered if Missus James had made matters worse. The rule kept Biggerman's temper at a slow boil. He was always on the lookout for an excuse to half-kill George.

No, there was no time to lose. Eliza knew she had to get her husband out of Kentucky and across the Ohio River to freedom this very night.

She pulled Beulah aside. "Your daddy and me has some work to do this evenin'. If you hear Mose, take care of him for me."

Beulah nodded without a speck of interest. Time was when she'd chatter on worse than a blue jay, but she'd barely spoken a word since her own husband had run off. Beulah did not seem to realize that Paul was better off free.

Eliza felt a tug at her apron. "Mammaw, where you and Pappaw goin'?" Shadrach's big eyes were full of questions. He was just four, but Beulah's oldest son was smart as a whip, much quicker than his older sister, Essie. Quicker than his mama, too.

"Oh, around the daisy." She pulled him on her lap. "I'll be back come morning, Shad. Now give your ol' Mammaw some sugar." Eliza loved him up until he giggled and squirmed.

When supper was over, Eliza sat on the edge of the bed and rocked Mose. She loved him fiercely and delighted to see his eyelids flutter open, even though she badly needed him to go to sleep. At last, he shivered all over and dozed off. She covered him up and kept a hand on his back for a long time.

She waited until Essie, Shad, Mary, and the twins, Meesh and Abe, fell asleep. Then she handed the heavy skillet to her daughter. "Beulah, honey, keep this by your bed. Happen you hear a noise, you fetch this skillet and clobber whatever it is, just as hard as you can."

Beulah nodded. Eliza wrapped her arms around her daughter and kissed her cheek. Then she covered George's mouth, took him by the hand, and led him out the door.

They made their way to the creek by starlight, and the cold grew sharper than needles. George seemed to understand the need for quiet. When Eliza took her hand from his mouth, he didn't make a sound. "Lord, just let me get him safe to the other side," she prayed.

For the next two miles, they followed the creek. Once, a deer crashed through the underbrush, and Eliza's heart nearly stopped. She looked behind her more than ahead, and she guided George back and forth across the meandering creek. She hoped to throw the patrollers off their scent.

She could hardly believe it when they reached the river and George found a skiff right away. He stumbled up against it so hard that he fell to his knees. He whimpered, and she patted his shoulder to chirk him up. How she loved him! He was so big and strong and kind.

The skiff was chained and locked to a thick post. Now, how to open the rusty padlock? Before she could fret, shrewdness lit George's face. He seized the post and pushed. He rocked it the other way and pulled the whole stake up out of the mud. He laid it in the bottom of the skiff with a proud smile.

She wiped away tears and settled George in the skiff. It took a struggle to shove it out into the water, but at last the skiff inched backward. George beamed when the boat rocked. Eliza wound strips of cloth through the oarlocks to muffle the screech of the oars. Then she clambered aboard, and they were afloat.

Mist danced along the top of the water. Eliza rowed upstream and tried to remember what she'd heard. Folks said there was a preacher who lived on a hill near Ripley. Mr. Rankin was his name. He would help slaves to a free country—if they could reach him. Mr. Rankin's dogs would not bark at a slave, for a wonder. Tales she'd heard through the grapevine said to walk right in the preacher's house because he never locked his door. Nobody had ever caught a runaway who got to Mr. Rankin's, neither. He must be a praying man, for sure. All she had to do was find the house once they landed.

Before long, the skiff struck the opposite shore. Eliza stepped out onto the riverbank and turned to help George. Before she could stop him, he jumped up, teetered, and splashed into the river. Thick mist swirled around her, and the darkness was complete.

The water's only knee deep. He must be nearby. She plunged in both arms up to her shoulders and searched in slow circles. The current tugged at her skirts and she stumbled. The water suddenly rose to her hips; she had stepped off a sandbar. If George did the same, he'd go under, and he could not swim. She had to find him fast, but where was he?

She risked a desperate whisper. "George!"

No answer. Frantic now, she leaned over so far that the front of her dress was soaked. She floundered every which way, but just like that, he was gone.

To come so close to freedom! A sob choked her. She raised a hand to smother her grief, and her fingertips brushed something—cloth. She lunged for it, missed, lunged again, and pulled blindly for all she was worth. Then the mist lifted and she saw that the heavy, wet bundle was George.

She dragged him to shore. He retched and spluttered. Water streamed from his eyes and nose, and she slapped him on the back. She struggled to lift him to his feet; the wind stiffened their wet clothes. George's teeth chattered, but he was alive, thank the Lord.

"Don't make another sound. Be still!" Two shadowy forms glided to her side. "Sam, get the skiff."

"Got it, Cal."

A voice close to her ear said, "Come with us. We'll help you."

Her eyes adjusted to the darkness, and Eliza saw a young white boy.

She shook her head and pointed at George. "Just him," she whispered. The other boy took Eliza's arm, but she whispered, "No."

"See here, ma'am, we have to move!"

"I can't go." She wrung her hands. "He fell in the river. He . . . he's feeble-minded." She added, "Biggerman, he gonna kill my George."

"Biggerman?" The big boys looked at each other. "Better come with us," the one called Cal urged.

"I got more family over to home." She would not cry now. "I'll come back by and by. Please, take him on to Canada for me."

"If you are going back, go now." Sam held the skiff steady for her.

She hesitated. It was so quick! She tiptoed to kiss George's cheek. "Lord keep you, George. I'll come back. I love you." With that, she turned blindly to the skiff.

Sam helped her embark and pushed the skiff off the sandbar. She huddled in her wet dress and let the current carry her downstream, with just the tip of an oar to steer.

The boys led George away. He turned back once. Twice. Just before they entered the woods, he shook free and cupped both hands around his mouth. "I love you, too." His husky whisper carried over the water and broke Eliza's heart.

By the time she reached home, she was cold to her very bones. Tears coursed down her cheeks with each strangled cough.

No one stirred when she opened the cabin door. Beulah lay

flat on her back in the bed with baby Mose clasped to her chest. She slept dead to the world.

Eliza stirred the fire. While she waited for the pot of water to boil, she picked a mess of sage from the bush outside her door. The leaves were small this late in the year, but fresh-picked sage always worked best for a cough. She tied the leaves in a scrap of stained muslin and placed it in a bowl. After she poured water over the bag, she covered the bowl with a chipped saucer.

The fire crackled. Her shoes would soon dry. She could easily excuse their dampness if need be, but her muddy, wet dress would be harder to explain. She turned it inside out and decided to let it dry on her. To ward off the chill, she filled the washtub with the rest of the hot water and soaked her feet.

When the sage tea had steeped, Eliza added a dribble of honey. She closed her weary eyes and inhaled the fragrant steam. Then she picked up the bowl in both hands and sipped the healing tea.

"Where's Pappaw at, Mammaw?"

Eliza jumped and tea slopped. Shad stood at her elbow. She did not know how to answer him.

"He with my daddy now?"

She had never seen such big, knowing eyes on a child. A lump came up in her throat but she forced a scowl. "You hush your mouth. Don't you never say that again, you hear me?"

Shad nodded. He hugged her neck. "I'm glad you come back," he whispered.

Oh, she loved this grandchild, but he was too smart for his own good. She gave him a sip of tea and sent him back to bed.

Daybreak, and there were still the cows for Beulah to milk. Eliza couldn't bear to wake her. Tired as she was, she padded barefoot through the wet grass to the cowshed.

The three cows turned their heads to watch her as they chewed their cud. With a groan, Eliza settled onto the milking stool and burrowed her head in the cow's warm flank. Streams of milk zinged into the pail.

"Milking mighty late, ain't you, Ol' Ugly?"

Eliza never missed a pull. "No, sir."

Laban Biggerman rose from the next pen. "How come that pretty daughter of yourn ain't milking this morning? She sick?"

"Yes, sir," Eliza fibbed. Thank the good Lord Beulah wasn't milking today. She coughed and wiped her nose. "We all be sick."

"Well, I'll go tell her I hope she feels better." He brushed soiled straw from his clothes and left the shed.

Before she finished milking the second cow, he strode back to her side. "Where's your man?" he barked.

"Up to the house."

Biggerman grabbed her by the neck and raised her off the stool to face him. "You know he ain't." He shook her. "He's too stupid to run off by himself. You helped him, you—"

"What you mean?" she wailed. "George gone? Oh, my poor George, he musta fell in the branch and drownded! Help me find him!"

"Shut up!" The force of his blow knocked her halfway across the pen. The frightened cow bellowed and kicked the pail. Warm milk showered over Eliza's dress. "I know what you did. You took him to Uncle Johnny Rankin's house."

"I'm sick. You see how sick I am." Her jaw throbbed and she tasted blood. "I don't have the strength to find my poor George, wherever he got to." She crouched in the deep straw to hide her muddy skirts. "Oh, he's drownded, he's drownded! Lord, have mercy on his soul!"

"Good riddance to him!" Biggerman pointed at Eliza. "Get your lazy black hide to work. Since I don't have his brawn no more, I'll take the work out of you. Yes, and I'll make you pay for what you did."

When he was gone, Eliza unwound her kerchief and dabbed her puffed lip. Her mouth felt full; she spat out a bloody tooth. She packed the new gap with a strip of wadded cloth from her kerchief. Then she finished the milking.

When Eliza had set the cream to rise in the pantry, Missus James approached. Her eyes were swollen with weeping. "Oh, Eliza, why ever did you make Mr. Biggerman so angry?" She dabbed her tears with a wadded handkerchief.

How did her mistress know? Eliza rubbed her jaw. Sure enough, she could feel a welt where he had struck her. "It don't differ," she said.

Missus James's face went crimson. "He says George is gone and you helped him go! We've been so good to you! We never let him raise a hand to your George. Is this the way you repay us?"

A cloud of dust sifted past the window. Hoofbeats rang. Biggerman's red horse screamed as the spurs raked his sides. Eliza's spine stiffened. "Where's he gone?"

"Will you hush your sass and listen to me?" Missus James wrung her hands. Her daughters clung to their mother's skirt and glared at Eliza. "Biggerman's gone after the slave trader!"

"Lord, have mercy," Eliza moaned. She sank into a chair. "Who'll take care of Beulah and her little ones when I'm sold away?"

"Don't you see? He's not going to sell you." Missus James was crying in earnest now. "He's already talked to Mr. James. He's going to sell Beulah and her children to Mr. Adkins, over Germantown way."

The blood drained from Eliza's face. "My Mose, too?"

"He didn't say anything about him. Oh, what shall I . . . ?"

But Eliza was halfway across the yard. She flung open the cabin door. "Beulah!"

Her daughter stood at the stove, surrounded by her children. She jiggled Mose as she stirred the corn meal mush. She didn't respond.

"Beulah! I'm talking to you. Look at me!"

Slowly she turned her head.

"You're sold, you and your babies, to Mr. Adkins. Biggerman's gone there now." Eliza sobbed. "Lord, forgive me!"

For the first time since her husband, Paul, ran off, a spark of defiance flared in Beulah's eyes. That light gave Eliza hope. "Beulah, listen to me. You got to be careful. You take care of my grandbabies. They need you."

She heard a quivery sigh behind her, and there was Shad. Big tears rolled down his cheeks; young as he was, he knew "sold" meant something awful.

Her joints popped as she knelt and folded him in her arms. "Look ahere, Shad. You're Mammaw's big helper. Keep after your mama when she don't talk. Pester her until she says something." She stroked his head as his tears wet her dress front. "You teach your sisters and brothers how to get along. Tell them—" Dear God! There was so little time! "Tell them to say, 'No, ma'am' and 'Yes, sir.' Make sure they always take off their caps before they go in the big house."

It was no use. She could never say all she wanted to Shad. Instead, she bowed her head and prayed to God that He would keep her family safe.

Chapter 3

JOHNNY

"MOVE OVER, OLD SORREL." Johnny shoved the horse's tawny flank with his palm. He shooed the horses into the pasture and set to work cleaning their stalls, the last of his morning chores. With every stab of the pitchfork, he rehearsed what he would say to Father. By the time he had spread the clean straw, he knew he would win.

He washed up by the back door and barreled into the kitchen. Ibby, his eldest sister, threw up her hands. "Johnny! You'll make my cake fall!"

"What's got into you?" Mother wiped flour on her apron. "You've been moping around ever since supper last night."

So Mother had noticed. "Where's Father?"

"He's in the parlor," Ibby began, "but . . ."

Johnny tore down the hall, excited words tumbling over each other before he reached the doorway. "Father! I'm eleven now. It's time you made me a conductor. I promise I will never tell anyone about the slaves we help—"

"That's enough, Johnny!" Father's tone was sharp.

"—and I just know I can be a conductor on the Underground!" He rounded the corner and came face-to-face with Father and Thomas McCague. His heart thudded.

"Oh, Johnny." Father sounded weary. "Suppose somebody else had been here instead of Mr. McCague? You would have given us away."

After one stricken glance at Father, Johnny flushed and hung his head. "I'm sorry." His feet dragged as he left the room.

"I'm telling you, John, that boy, whew-ee!" Mr. McCague's laugh followed Johnny out the front door. "It's too bad he don't have the presence of mind that Lowry has. Now, there's a young man with a good head on his shoulders."

That settled it. Now he'd never see a fugitive slave, much less be a conductor. Johnny sat under his hedge apple tree and rested his chin on his knees. When would he learn to hold his tongue? He stared at the town of Ripley, spread out below him. Up the river and down, and over in Kentucky as far as he could see, there lived not one person who believed in him.

"Oh, there you are! Wherever did you go last night, Johnny?" Mandy bundled her skirts and sat down beside him.

He shrugged.

"Well, I've been spinning all morning," Mandy said. "I need some fresh air. Will you take a walk with me?"

"Why don't you go with Lowry?"

Mandy answered slowly, "Why, I wanted to go with you. But if you don't feel like walking . . ."

"I guess I do." He stood and helped her to her feet.

When they reached town, they wandered past the church toward the river. Johnny's spirits rose; it was hard to stay gloomy on such a fine October day. He hefted a smooth flat stone—just right. Mandy made a good audience as he skipped it across the water. She even clapped when he broke his old record of seven skips. Disappointment faded until he thought about Lowry. He hurled the next stone so hard that water splashed back at them.

"What's bothering you, Johnny?"

"No matter what I do, it turns out wrong," he burst out. "But no matter what Lowry does, it turns out right. Everyone thinks the world of Lowry, but I'm just a pest and a tattletale." He picked up a dead branch and slashed at the weeds along the riverbank.

Mandy's eyes were grave. "No, you're not. Why, just this morning, Lowry said you—"

"Lowry!" He snapped the branch in two. "He has no use for me. I don't even think he likes me."

"Oh, yes, he does!" Mandy clasped her hands. "He does, I know it. And as for what people think of Lowry, has he ever told you about his first year at Lane Seminary? No? Why, it's a wonder he ever made up his mind to be a preacher. In fact, he's still not certain he can do it."

Rock-solid Lowry, unsure of himself? It hardly seemed possible to Johnny. He tried to sort out what Mandy was saying.

She guessed his thoughts. "Lowry doubts himself all the time. He said we couldn't tell anyone we were engaged until he had found a church, but I think he was really too shy. He was afraid everyone would say he couldn't provide for me." Mandy's face lit up with joy at the idea of sharing a home with Lowry.

"I wish you weren't going to marry him."

She touched his shoulder gently. "I love him, Johnny."

He kicked a stone into the river.

What Mandy said next surprised him. "Johnny, I want to thank you for all the flowers you've picked for me."

He stared. "How did you find out?"

"I saw you leave them one morning. Spring beauties, violets, black-eyed Susans . . . every season you've brought me the prettiest kinds. No one else has ever given me flowers." She smiled. "Not even Lowry."

He chirked up a bit. Small wonder Lowry had never thought to pick flowers for Mandy. He was always too worried, but now Johnny knew why.

"When Lowry and I are married, you'll be my brother," she pointed out. "And we'll live with your family until Lowry gets a church of his own."

"But then you'll move away."

"Maybe not," she said, but her face clouded. "Even if that should happen, I'll still be your sister. And don't forget, there is One who will never leave or forsake you. He knows what you can do."

Johnny stopped in his tracks. He understood about God, but what did she mean by that last part? Did Mandy know a secret about the Underground? He opened his mouth to ask her, but she was already too far ahead. He caught up with her.

"Mandy, do . . . ?"

"Will you still pick flowers for me, Johnny?" Her kind, blue eyes made him forget everything else. He managed a smile and a nod, and the bright sunshine warmed their backs as they walked home.

Johnny would recall the sun's warmth many times during the wicked winter that followed. After a summer-long drought and fine fall weather, the bitter north wind screamed and a white shroud of snow enveloped Ripley. The temperature plunged, and the skim of ice along the shores of the river thickened daily. By December, the newspaper said the Ohio River was frozen solid from the Mississippi to its source. All river travel ceased, except when foolhardy young men dared each other to drive their sleighs out on the ice, or when Kentucky slaves crossed the ice bridge to freedom.

Spring's advent was subtle. The blue jays returned near Johnny's twelfth birthday, a couple of days before February ended. By mid-March, the snow had softened and grayed. New green growth crept up from the forest floor. Rivulets of water ran everywhere. Old-timers groused that they did not know which was worse, ice or mud.

Now Johnny and his friends, Hugh Willey and Newt Poage, tried to predict just when the ice would break up. They had loitered every day at the river's edge, checking the progress of the sun. Pores had opened, and the boys watched the sluggish water gurgle up and ooze over the ice.

"Any day now." Hugh nodded wisely.

Johnny chuckled and flung the twig he had sharpened with his Barlow knife so that it stuck deep in the mud. "Everyone knows that. The question is, which day?"

"I say Friday," Newt said in a rush.

Hugh was almost as quick. "Tomorrow for me!"

Last choice! Johnny pulled a wry mouth. He leaned toward the ice, considering.

"You get back from there this instant, Johnny Rankin! That ice is not safe when the pores open up."

Johnny turned in surprise. A flock of bright-feathered church ladies roosted on a nearby front porch. "Yes, ma'am," he said meekly, but inside he was boiling mad. Did they really believe that a boy who had practically grown up on the river would touch a toe to rotten ice? Nobody had ventured out on it for almost two days. He backed away but shot a glance at Hugh and Newt. Both boys grinned and tsk-tsked their fingers at him.

He squinted at the sun's glare on the ice and shrugged. "I call tonight."

Newt wagged his head. "It'll never break up that fast."

"Hey, Johnny!" The voice came from up the riverbank, behind a hedge of bushes near the road.

"Sounds like Sam," Hugh said.

"Checking the ice, fellows?" Sam strode into view. "Johnny, can you help me? I need to sweep the mud out of the sanctuary.

I wish to goodness people would use the boot scraper before they go in." He was the sexton of Father's church.

"I suppose." Johnny answered his brother without much enthusiasm and waved to his friends. "Remember, I spoke for tonight!" He fell in step with Sam.

"You think the ice will break up tonight?" Sam teased.

"O'course not, but Hugh and Newt spoke first."

"Well, don't fret, you could be right. Besides, you know what they say."

"What?"

Sam's face was droll as he mimicked Lowry's bossy tone. "'If you want to know what's going on in Ripley, go ask Johnny.'"

Johnny threw a good-natured shove that barely budged Sam; he was ever so much bigger. The brothers quibbled about the ice while they swept the front walk and filled the wood box at the church. Then Johnny tackled the dried mud in the sanctuary with the edge of a stubby broom. Sam neatened the hymnals in the pew racks and dusted the pews, carefully tracing the walnut scrollwork that Mother's brother, Uncle William, had carved.

When he finished the pews, Sam took the slender glass chimneys from each tin sconce along the walls and handed them down to Johnny. Johnny was too short to reach the chimneys himself, but it was his job to wipe the soot from inside the glass because Sam's hand was too meaty to fit. Meanwhile, Sam dislodged the old candle stubs, scraped away the melted wax, and inserted new tallow candles. It took a long time to make sure the church would be properly lighted on Sunday.

The boys swept the floor clean of candle shavings, wood fragments, dirt, and dust. Then they inspected their work. "No use to scrub the floor until the mud outside dries," Johnny said hopefully.

"Nope," Sam agreed with a broad grin. The peaceful sanctuary shone from narthex to chancel. "Thanks, Johnny. That's a job well done." Sam craned his neck to make sure they were alone before he spoke in a hushed voice. "One thing's certain. If the ice breaks up tonight, we'll have no more business for a long time."

Johnny knew he meant the Underground. He sighed; his birthday had come and gone, and he had not yet seen a fugitive. "Maybe not," he ventured.

"You know no one's been out on the ice for a couple of days. It's over, mark my words." Sam pushed open the door. "And I can use the rest."

They heard a muddy squelch. "Afternoon, Samuel Gardiner. Afternoon, John Thompson. Been cleaning the church?" Mrs. McCague asked.

She was the only person in Ripley who called everyone by his full name. "Good afternoon, Aunt Kittie. Yes, ma'am, we have," Johnny said. Though she was no relation to the Rankin family, they addressed her with the familiar term of respect.

Sam caught Johnny's eye. "Biscuit-cutters," he whispered, and he gestured at Aunt Kittie's shoes. Both boys hid a smile as she wobbled past with pattens clipped to her shoes. The metal rings worked like inch-high stilts and kept her dainty shoes out of the muck. How she kept her balance, Johnny could not fathom.

Proper as she was, Aunt Kittie had a heart as big as her home state of Kentucky. Kentuckians and Ohioans alike loved and respected her. The Rankins were among the handful who knew she and her husband had sheltered many slaves on the Underground.

A flurry of hoofbeats caught Johnny's attention.

Sam turned and heaved a happy sigh. Agnes Dickens rode down the street on her black saddle mare, Raven. The mare pranced until the young lady's curly hair bobbed in rhythm. Her russet riding costume and matching hat brought out the stormy blue of her eyes. Johnny could easily understand why half the young men in Ripley were in love with Agnes, though of course Mandy was prettier.

"She's a beauty," Sam said reverently.

Johnny snickered. "If anybody else said that out loud, I'd be embarrassed, but I know you mean Raven."

"What?" Sam's quick wit left him for once. "I don't see why Arch Hopkins sells his best horses. You'd think he'd want to keep Bonny's daughter, much in love as he is with his sweet dapple-gray."

The glossy mare's hooves fairly twinkled through the mud. If Johnny would let him, Sam would watch Raven all day. He loved horses. Johnny could take them or leave them, but he had to admit that Raven was indeed a beauty.

Cr-ack!

Both boys jumped at a sharp report that echoed like a gunshot. Raven shied and tossed her head in alarm. She fought the bit and curveted in frustration; she wanted to run. Instead, she reared. Agnes leaned into the mare and stuck tight to the saddle as they neared vertical. Johnny moved instinctively to help her, but Sam caught his arm. "Watch," he said.

Sure enough, Raven plunged back to earth at her rider's command. Agnes praised the mare, and Raven responded with a beautifully collected jog.

"She sure can ride, and sidesaddle at that," Sam said. "There's no other lady in Ripley who could handle Raven." He watched until Raven was out of sight and then punched Johnny's arm. "Maybe you're right about the ice. Sounds like it's breaking up after all. Race you!"

They picked up their heels and sprinted. After the endless winter, it felt good to gulp in deep breaths of balmy air as they ran. Johnny dashed two blocks straight down Mulberry Street and was just getting warmed up when a shop door swung open. Mr. McCague and Robert Patton, the burliest man in Ripley, stepped right into his path. Johnny swerved and narrowly missed a collision. He braced himself for the outburst, and true to his nickname, Jolly Bob chortled. "Hey, Johnny Rankin, what's going on, young fellow?"

Excitement made Johnny's voice crack. "The ice is breaking up!"

He and Sam sped on. Before they were out of earshot, they heard Mr. McCague comment, "I declare, that boy is a regular Paul Revere!"

Smothered giggles checked his speed again. He glanced aside and saw a bevy of his female schoolmates. They ducked their heads to whisper as he passed, all but Mary Ann Hay. Coppery braids flashed in the sun as she tipped her head to one side and studied him, the same way she always did. There were secrets in her eyes.

A crowd of excited men and boys had gathered on the riverbank below Front Street. Johnny stopped at Tom Collins's cabinet shop just long enough to holler, "The ice is breaking up! Come see!"

Poor Mr. Collins was nearly deaf, but he poked his shock of white hair out the door to see what all the commotion was about. Johnny gestured at the ice and pantomimed breaking a stick. Mr. Collins's eyes widened, and he stepped down to the river with them.

Sure enough, a long fissure snaked halfway across the river. The edges ground together with a sound that made Johnny's teeth hurt. He remarked with satisfaction, "Well, that's it!"

"What's that you say?" Mr. Collins cupped a hand to his ear. His English accent made even the simplest sentence sound formal.

Mr. McCague bellowed, "No boats now!" Broken-up chunks of ice could capsize a boat, and everyone there knew it.

Mr. Collins snapped to attention. He stared hard at something. Mr. McCague touched his shoulder. Mr. Collins nodded upriver in response. Everyone glanced toward a distant knot of willows that hugged the outlet of Red Oak Creek. Johnny strained to make out Zeke Means.

There was a flash, a reflection of bright sunlight. Perhaps Zeke had cut a plug of tobacco with his long, wicked knife. Johnny remembered that Zeke's young giant of a brother, Luke, had once beaten up Lowry when they were in grammar school. Zeke himself had savagely cowhided Benjamin Templeton, a freedman who had boarded with the Rankins while he attended Ripley College. Now Zeke and his brother had a new business—slave-catching.

Johnny edged closer to Sam while the men exchanged sober glances. Then to everyone's surprise, Mr. Collins stage-whispered, "He'll be waiting a long time." He smiled at the cracked ice.

It took all Johnny's will to smother a laugh at the slave-catcher's misfortune. Luckily, Sam's stomach growled. "Wonder what's for supper? I'm starved."

"Just like always," Johnny said. The men laughed, Jolly Bob the loudest, and the boys headed home with light hearts.

All during supper, Johnny told his prediction about the ice to anyone who would listen. Then, while the girls cleared the table, he squared his shoulders and tried Father again for the umpteenth time that winter. If he could not take a fugitive to the next station, could he at least see one? The next one?

Father smiled and said, "We'll see. Although if the ice breaks up tonight as you say, there'll be no fugitives for many nights to come."

As he lay in bed later that night, Johnny recalled the long, cold winter. Seemed like the only thing he'd done right was to pick today for the ice to break up, but now even that had turned out wrong: no ice, no fugitives for him to conduct.

The ice creaked and moaned until sleep was nigh impossible. Nonetheless, he must have dozed because a mighty roar like thunder roused him just before midnight. He knew the roar meant his prediction had come true. Before he fell back to sleep, he resigned himself to the cold, hard fact—it might be months before another fugitive slave came to his house.

Chapter 4

ELIZA

THE DEEP SNOW THAT had blanketed the hills for months was melting fast. Eliza stood in her doorway one evening and watched a rabbit sink down a good inch with each hop. The rabbit sat up on its haunches and sniffed the air. Cautious whiskers twitched. The next instant, a shadow struck the rabbit's neck. A great-horned owl swooped away with its prey clutched in sure talons as blood splattered the snow.

Eliza shivered. An arc of water sparkled as she emptied her pail. Was the owl some kind of sign? She made up her mind to study on the omen a while. She clutched her red shawl and shut the door.

Three nights later, big patches of bare ground made a pattern in the snow. Warm wind teased with the promise of spring, but Eliza's heart ached. Now she knew what the owl sign meant. Biggerman hadn't stopped at selling away Beulah and her children last fall. A slave trader was coming tomorrow to buy Eliza and Mose and ship them to New Orleans. She had overheard Missus James wail, "In the name of Christian charity, please don't sell Eliza!" But Biggerman had laughed and said it was already arranged. Mr. James was away, buying horses down in Lexington, so there would be no help from him. Besides, the master had had so much trouble with Eliza and her family that he'd be glad to get rid of them.

"Few more hours and I'll be in the same fix as that little old rabbit," she mourned. She looked up at the Drinking Gourd and the North Star before clouds sailed across them. Late March. Likely she had waited too long. Folks said the ice on the Ohio River was so full of air holes that it looked like a honeycomb. No one dared set foot on it now, but she had no choice. Rotten ice or no, if she was going to run away, she must leave tonight.

Over at the big house, the windows were black squares. The white folks had put out the candle and gone to bed early without a care in the world. A film of angry tears clouded her vision.

A soft sigh from Mose calmed her. She would go away, and so would he. He was all she had left. Eliza tucked her herbs and seeds in her kerchief and retied it around her head. She made a sling out of her shawl as she rocked the cradle with her toe. The broken runner thunked, but Mose was used to that rhythm. He slept with his rump in the air and fingers curled over his snub nose as he sucked his thumb.

She lifted him out of the cradle. Mose curled into the warm nest of the sling, and she rubbed his back. Once he went to sleep, only thunder would awaken him.

Well, we're ready. Since God had seen fit to freeze over the Ohio River, she would walk across it to freedom or drown trying. "Now, Lord, You take care of us," she whispered, and she stole into the night.

The creek outside Eliza's door foamed and ate away at the ice until there was just a razor-edged strip of white. The water was much too wide to cross now, and it flared out even more as she got closer to the big river. Mud coated her shoes and made each step along the water's edge a struggle.

Her journey took so long that the river patrollers were surely drunk and incapacitated by now—cold comfort, but a boon nonetheless. After two hours, Eliza was sopping wet from the melting snow that slithered over her from the tree branches above her head. Her cold fingers were locked under Mose's sleeping frame. For the last quarter of an hour, she had heard the river. She stopped short when the Ohio came into view.

Snowmelt roared down the hillsides, crashed on the river-bank, sloshed into the air, and cascaded back to the ground. The yellow runoff foamed over the ice until it was half a foot deep in spots. With the muddy water above and the swollen surge below, the ice on the river shivered like an old man. Worse yet, ice that had hugged the Kentucky shore now ended in a jagged shelf eight impossible feet beyond her reach. The swift current would knock her down and pull her and Mose under if she tried to wade out there. It was too late to cross.

Eliza leaned against a sycamore and considered her chances. Drowning was better than what awaited her if she gave up and went home. She'd never make it back before her master and mistress awoke. Biggerman would half-kill her before the slave trader arrived to sell her off to the big slave markets in New Orleans. What if she were sold to a cotton plantation? She shuddered. An overseer's whip would flay her skin, and one day Mose's, if they failed to pick a hundred pounds of cotton a day. The truth was, she could be whipped if she so much as looked at a white man wrong, even when she picked her share of cotton.

Maybe she should have tried to see Beulah and the grand-babies one more time before she ran off. She hesitated, sorely tempted.

She could not risk a visit. Mose was here now, and she must go on, even though the ice bridge in front of her melted with every passing second. Worse yet, fog seeped along the river bottoms so that she could hardly see. Her faith dwindled smaller than a sparrow, no more than a fluff of feathers and a heartbeat, and her heart sank.

Then the fog drifted and she glimpsed the Ohio shore. Free-dom awaited just a half mile away. God had brought her this far; surely to goodness she could jump that first eight feet . . .

"Lass, you'll not make it!"

She nearly jumped out of her skin. A man walked toward her through the fog.

"Have some sense! I've been checking the ice for two days, and it's about to break up. You'll go down like a stone." Angry sparks snapped in his eyes.

She backed toward the river and squeezed Mose tight. A wail escaped the folds of the red shawl.

The man's mouth fell open. "A baby?" Precious seconds passed. When he spoke again, his voice was gentle. "You come along with me. I'll help you."

She glanced behind him—he was alone. His cabin poked out of the fog on the hilltop. Should she trust this man? Angry one minute, gentle the next; how could she know for sure? *So weary, Lord. So weary.* She stared at the ice for a long minute before she trudged after him.

At the cabin door, she slipped off her muddy shoes and stepped inside. Shadows wavered along the cabin walls as the fire danced. The first thing Eliza looked for was the man's broom. It was worn to a slant and propped in a corner away from the bedstead, just like back home. The superstition went that if a broom leaned against the bed, it meant bad luck. She relaxed a notch but kept her guard up while the old man tried to put her at ease.

"Name's Asa Anderson. There's been no one but me here for many a year."

Suspicion sharpened her voice. "Got no wife or children?"

His mouth drooped. "I lost my wife and baby in childbirth long ago."

Eliza believed him—almost. She saw thread, yarn, and a darning gourd strewn over the white-scoured table. She pointed. "You mendin' those stockings yourself?"

"Aye." He picked one up, and Eliza saw he had indeed done it himself—a crooked darn showed. He tossed the stocking aside. "Rest a bit," he said.

What comfort to sink into a chair near the fire! She fished Mose from the clammy shawl. He never stirred as she clasped him tightly and stretched her wet stockings toward the fire. The clock on the mantel tapped a silver finger. Eliza's eyes rolled back and she almost nodded off in the blessed warmth.

The old man retrieved the shawl from her lap and draped it over a chair to dry. He handed her a stoneware bowl. "Have some cornbread. Let me dandle your little one while you eat."

"No, sir . . ." She drew back.

"Half a moment, only." His hands shook.

Then she knew. It must have been years since he'd held a baby; maybe he never had. She gave Mose to him.

Mr. Anderson gathered him up like a greedy horse takes sugar. He smiled while the baby's fists flailed. When Mose whimpered, a steady stream of baby talk soon quieted him. Then Mr. Anderson walked out of sight to the other room, and Eliza caught a hint of cedar. A short time later, the old man reappeared and surrendered her boy, now bundled in something soft and warm.

"What's this on my baby?" She fingered a coverlet creased by the passing years. Maybe it was white once, but the color had aged to cream.

Mr. Anderson waved a hand. "I have no need of that old thing. It's good warm wool. He's welcome to it." He took a pail from the bench. "Feed him now." Cool air circulated into the room before the door swung shut.

Eliza chewed the greasy cornbread and stroked the coverlet while her son nursed. When he was asleep, she laid him down and shucked off her cotton petticoat. She tied it over one shoulder and settled Mose, thickly swaddled, in the makeshift sling. Then she waited for the old man to return.

When was the last time she had sat still like this? She struggled to stay awake. Mr. Anderson's stocking, now—he'd made a mess of it. She clucked her tongue and worked the darning gourd into the toe. When she had unraveled his clumsy darn, she whipped a framework of thread from top to bottom across the hole. Then she wove new yarn from side to side under experienced fingers. She bit the yarn in two, tied it off, drew out the gourd, and rolled the mended stocking with its mate.

Where was that man? He'd been gone a mighty long time. What if he had gone to turn her in for a reward so he could keep her baby? It took all her will to keep from bolting. She let out her pent-up breath in relief when his boots clattered on the porch.

"I cut a white cedar bough and brushed out our tracks. No one will know you're here." His eyes crinkled with pleased surprise when he noticed the mended stocking. He handed a gourd of fresh water to Eliza. She drank it down and wiped her mouth on her sleeve.

"Do you know where Mr. Rankin lives?"

"Aye." Mr. Anderson brushed back a curtain and pointed to a speck of light upriver. "That's his place."

"Right there?" It did not seem far. "How long you figure it'll take us?"

The clock tapped. "Lass, what are you saying?" The old man's voice cracked. "You must not cross that rotten ice. Think of your baby!"

"I am thinkin' of him. He's got to be free." Eliza's heart pounded. Would this man try to keep her here?

A sound quavered on the air, like somebody had knocked one thin icicle off the roof. Mr. Anderson cupped a hand to his ear. "What's that?"

She heard it again, like the ghostly chime of a faraway church bell. Eliza knew what it meant. Biggerman had set his bloodhounds on her. She snatched up the red shawl and threw it over Mose.

She made it halfway to the door before Mr. Anderson blocked her. "Under the bedstead, quickly!"

She wanted to run so bad her legs shook. A hiding place was not enough. Only freedom would do now. She tried to make him understand. "I helped my man run off. I left my girl and her babies. The slave trader's gonna sell me and this boy down the river. Please let us go."

Mr. Anderson's chin sunk to his chest. Eliza remembered his wife and baby, stolen away from him so long ago. It seemed like forever before he raised his head and sighed. Then he opened the door, and Eliza shot through it like a sparrow out of a cage.

They skidded down the muddy hill. Mr. Anderson stopped at a ramshackle shed and emerged with a cedar plank. A knotted rope was threaded through a hole at one end. "I use this to cross the creek," he told her. Eliza nodded as he wound the rope around her hand several times. "Perhaps it may catch if you go down, and you can pull yourself out."

"Don't you worry none. The good Lord will help us. Thank you. God bless you."

"Godspeed, lassie," Mr. Anderson whispered. "Take care of him." The fog swallowed him as he climbed the hill.

Eliza tucked her red shawl close about Mose. They were on their own again. The hounds' constant dirge was barely audible above the roar of the water. She stretched out the plank and let it fall on the ice. The other end she ground into the mud with her heel.

"It ain't much of a bridge, Lord," she muttered. Sweat trickled down her back and her cold feet worked no better than two blocks of wood, but she soon reached the ice.

She supported Mose with the crook of one arm and pulled the plank after her. "Lord, keep helpin' us now, You hear?" she pleaded. The thought of the light in Mr. Rankin's house over yonder encouraged her even as the thought of the hounds struck terror in her heart.

Her shoes bumped over frozen wind-ripples and through slushy pools. The solid rope was wonderful to hold, especially when she remembered what lay beneath the ice. *Don't think about the cold water!* she scolded herself. Sweat stung her eyes, and she felt as steamy as a Kentucky summer. Cold water! That sounded mighty—

The ice buckled. Eliza's right knee smashed a spider-web dent in the thin crust. How long before she drowned? She peeked under her shoulder.

Wonder of wonders, she had not broken clean through, after all. The toe of her left shoe still rested on the sunken imprint; water bubbled up around the edges. She scraped a place free of slush and set the plank's end as far ahead as she dared. Gingerly she pulled herself upright. She eased her foot from the crack and started off again.

At times Eliza could see her feet through the fog; sometimes she scooted blind. Always the icy edges of her skirt scratched her ankles. She hurt in a hundred places, and her wet clothes hung heavy. Mr. Anderson's greasy cornbread was a lump in her insides. It was a wonder she kept it down. Every time the ice heaved, her stomach did, too.

How far? Eliza glanced up from her feet toward the shore. The next instant she stepped wrong. Quicker than a flash, the ice up-ended. Instinctively, she whipped Mose's sling over her head and shoved him away. Then—bless Mr. Anderson!—she pulled the plank across the hole in the ice and hung on.

Trouble was, Eliza was waist-deep and sinking in water colder than the grave. She gulped air and water and flailed her legs to fight the current, but it dragged at her heavy skirts and threatened to pull her under the ice. There was no breath left to sob, no time to say prayers. She could see Mose lying there on the ice just out of reach, but she could not save her son.

Then the toe of her shoe scraped a sandbar. With a mighty

effort, she pushed off from the sandbar and hitched her knee over the plank until she sat astride it. She lowered her shoulder to the ice and rolled. Her other leg came out of the water. She collapsed on her back and panted for a moment. At last, she threw out her hand and dragged Mose to her.

For a long time her wheezing drowned out all other sounds. Leastways she did not hurt now. She was so cold she could not feel a thing, but all she cared about was Mose. He lay so still! She clasped him to her and dug her heels in the slush. When she had scooted on her back a ways beyond the hole, she struggled to her feet.

She looked back to retrieve the plank, but it was gone, taken by the current. Then the mist parted. Victory! The Ohio shore was ten feet away.

"Oh, my Lord!" she whispered. "Glory, glory!" Five steps through shallow water and they were free, but she could not stop to rejoice. Was Mose all right?

As she clawed at the icy shawl, she saw a shadow. A hand clapped her shoulder like a talon. Trouble piled on top of trouble—Eliza could not bear it. She moaned and sank to her knees. Somebody wrenched her right arm high behind her back.

The trick to bearing pain was to think about something good; she thought about Mose and how much she loved him. By the time her captor hauled her to her feet, she was beyond fear. Then he spun her to face him, and Eliza knew she would never escape. He was huge.

"Scared ya, din I?" He whiskey-slurred his words. "Thought you was a goner jus' now. Zeke Means, at your service. Glad to meet you." He laughed so hard that he hacked.

She wondered dully whether Mose were alive or dead, but it didn't really matter now. He was lost to Eliza, sure as the world. The distant baying took on a frantic note; the bloodhounds had picked up her scent. This man would collect his reward money, easy as you please, and Eliza would be bound for New Orleans before the sun rose.

The big man shook out a rope and held a loop in his teeth. As he grabbed for her hand, he jabbed Eliza's red shawl. An indignant howl of pain startled them both. Eliza nearly shouted, "Hallelujah!" Her baby was alive.

Zeke's face was a study. He ripped away the shawl and revealed Mose, still neatly wrapped in Mr. Anderson's sodden coverlet. The red shawl slipped from the slave-catcher's fingers and landed like a splotch of blood on the snow. "How did you carry a baby across that ice?"

Eliza paid him no mind. "You's all right, shh, shh," she soothed her baby. She hugged Mose fiercely. Seemed like she could bear whatever happened now. She faced her new master.

The man's mouth worked, but no sound came out. Whatever he was trying to say came mighty hard. Finally, he got it out. "Woman, you've earned your freedom."

White man's words. Just listen, no need to understand—that's how she got by. She nodded slightly to show she was paying attention and lifted the sling over her head.

"You've earned your freedom," Zeke Means repeated slowly. After the longest time, he added, "But you're the only one."

She heard what he said this time, but it didn't mean anything. All she knew was her son needed help this minute. She chafed his hands and feet. "My boy," she whispered. She drew him out of the petticoat sling, dropped it beside the red shawl, and wrapped the coverlet tight around him. With shaky fingers, she unbuttoned the front of her dress and snuggled Mose against her heart.

Lord, have mercy, she had clean forgot that white man! Here she had undone her dress right in front of him. She cringed and peeked over her shoulder, but he was gone. What had he said? "You've earned your freedom." Her knees trembled. The slave-catcher was gone, and she and Mose were free.

Reckon she didn't need to be told twice. She turned her back on slavery forever and set off through the mud for the red brick house high above Ripley.

The steps up the hill were steep and seemed endless. Eliza lost sight of the lantern until she reached the crest of the hill, and the house sprang up before her. She heard a snuffle and a whine, and a damp nose brushed her palm. The Rankin family dog licked Eliza's fingers and trotted beside her to the door. The dog did not bark, just as Eliza had always heard through the grapevine. She pried off her muddy shoes, picked them up, and opened the door.

Stepping into the tiny vestibule, she tiptoed down a narrow hallway that led to the kitchen. A faint glow revealed the box stove. She poked the fire to a blaze, tucked her shoes under the stove to dry, and thawed her frozen hands. Bean soup simmered in a kettle pushed to the back of the stove. She stirred it and opened the warming oven. There sat a pan of biscuits wrapped in a dishcloth.

A pitcher of water rested in a china bowl on the dry sink and a folded towel lay to one side. Eliza unwrapped Mose. She dabbed her baby's face clean and chafed his hands and feet until he whimpered. She rummaged through a ragbag and fashioned a diaper for her son. Then she fed him and snuggled him close. When he was fast asleep, she bedded him down.

How good it felt to mop her own face and neck! She plunged and thawed her cold hands in the bowl and scrubbed away all the mud. As she hung up the sodden coverlet to dry, she wondered if heaven might be this way.

Why doesn't someone come out to see what all this noise is about? She stood by the stove and with the biscuits sopped up hot bean soup straight from the kettle until both were gone. The simple meal warmed her through. She drank a full dipper of water and wanted no more than this.

Well, yes she did. She'd come into a spotless house, and she meant to leave it that way. She heated water to scrub the kettle. When she was done, a pool of melted water from her dress shimmered on the floor. Soon as she could wring out her dress so it wouldn't drip anymore, she would mop that up, too. She reckoned there was no one happier than she was right now. Yes, she had redded up someone else's kitchen, but of her own free choice.

Footsteps sounded on the stairs, and a short man with graying hair shuffled into the room. The candle he carried trailed a wisp of smoke. He yawned, "See here, Sam, don't we have enough of these late night commotions without you sneaking down for a bite to eat after midnight? Now, bank that fire and get back to bed."

Startled, Eliza faced the man whom she'd blessed in her prayers every night, the man who had sent George on to freedom. He was fully dressed, and slighter than she'd expected. If anybody had slept through her kitchen banging, the boom of his words had put an end to that. She waited for him to notice her.

"Why, I beg your pardon, Auntie!" he said. Eliza almost laughed, but then she heard a terrific crack and a long *cre-e-ak*, like a nail pulled from a coffin. The pastor shot a glance toward the front of the house—the ice was breaking up. Shock registered plainly. "How in the world did you get here?" he whispered.

"I done walked, Mr. Rankin."

There was a long pause. "Walked on what?"

"We come on the ice."

"We? Why, who else is here?" As Pastor Rankin scanned the room, Mose hiccupped in his sleep. The poor man nearly ran to the dry sink. He stood stock-still with his back to Eliza. Then he gingerly picked up the baby.

When he turned around, his cheeks glistened with tears. "The

Lord was with you." He cleared his throat. "No one can possibly come after you tonight. Mrs. Rankin will help you out of those wet things and tend to your baby. Rest here while I fetch her." He handed Mose to her and thought for a moment. "I believe my son would like to see you, too."

Eliza merely nodded, content to let somebody else take over. Nothing else mattered except that she and Mose were free at last.

Chapter 5

JOHNNY

"UNH?" JOHNNY OPENED one eye. The signal light shone in the window and framed Father's silhouette. "Time . . . build fire a'ready?"

"Shh. Want to see a refugee, Johnny? Skedaddle downstairs if you do."

He blinked. "A refugee?"

But Father was already whispering, "Cal, David, up like bucks. Work to do." Groans issued from the other bed.

Johnny slipped into his trousers and tucked in his shirt. He let his suspenders hang as he stuffed his feet into his boots. He squinted at Sam and Andy. They rolled over; even in their sleep they knew it wasn't their turn to build the morning fire.

His first runaway! He took the stairs two at a time. He conjured up an image of a fierce young man bulging with muscle. The fellow must be a lot braver than most to risk crossing the ice. Johnny hitched up his suspenders and went to meet him.

The kitchen was barely warm, but Johnny's cheeks burned. Ibby, Father, and Mother crowded around the table. Mother gently rocked baby Tappan to keep him quiet. Tenderhearted Ibby wept. They all moved aside to let him see.

At first, he thought that there must have been some mistake. A stout woman sat in front of him. Gray hair straggled from beneath her kerchief. Her skin was light, like a golden biscuit when it first begins to smell good. Her eyes were set so deep that he stared at her for several seconds before he realized she stared right back at him.

David and Cal clumped down the stairs, still half asleep. "How'd he get here?" Cal asked through a yawn.

"It's a woman," Father said, "and she crossed the ice."

The older boys stopped in their tracks to stare at Father, whose face was redder than Johnny had ever seen it. Ibby's thin shoulders shook, and Mother patted the old woman's shoulder with her free hand.

"She couldn't have," David said.

"But she did . . . and she carried her baby along."

For the first time, Johnny saw that the bundle in Mother's arms was not Tappan. He sidled up to Mother and gazed in wonder at the drowsy baby. A lump rose in his throat. "How?"

The woman's eyes were weary but she flashed a grin that revealed a missing tooth. "I just asked the good Lord for help. He done brought us here, me and this boy," she said.

"Your faith, Auntie . . ." Father shook his head. "Please tell us what happened."

The instant the slave began to speak, the kitchen and Johnny's family faded from his view. He saw only the woman as she slogged through ankle-deep mud and panted under the heavy load slung from her neck and shoulder. He hid with her among the sycamores as the runoff cascaded down the hills onto the ice. The river widened before his eyes but the ice remained the same size, even melted some. How did she cross? He could hardly wait to hear.

However, to his frustration, the woman stopped and squinted at Cal. "I done seen you before." She broke into an eager smile. "You one of the boys helped my man George on to Canada, last fall. He get on all right?"

Cal shot a swift glance at Father and ducked his head. "Yes, ma'am." His expression said plainly that she was crazy if she thought that he could recall one slave when he'd helped hundreds to freedom.

Johnny chewed his lip. "Auntie, the ice! What happened next?"

Then once again he inched across the ice with her while water sluiced over their shoe tops. The ghostly wail of the hounds in the distance raised gooseflesh on his arms. He could not catch his breath and fought the icy tug of the water when she broke through the ice. When she picked up her baby and scooted on her back, he barely restrained a cheer.

After she described her last few steps to the shore, she stopped. Johnny exhaled. Slowly the kitchen came back into focus. He noticed a red smear on his finger; he'd picked his lip until it bled.

What she had done was impossible, yet here she sat. Mother handed her a dipper of water, and she drank. She smacked her lips and said, "Well, sir, I was glad to step on dry land, but I like to jumped right out of my skin when that man grabbed my shoulder."

Father turned pale. "What man, Auntie?"

"Big ol' feller. Means, said his name was."

A log popped in the stove and a shower of red sparks snapped in the ash-pan. Father's words dropped like stones. "Zeke Means caught you?"

She nodded. "But when he saw my baby, he said, 'Woman, you've earned your freedom,' and he let me go."

Then Father moved like lightning. "Hurry, boys! Saddle Old Sorrell with Mother's saddle and get your horses ready. Let down the fence and get away from here before Means has a change of heart!" He turned to the woman. "Did he say anything else?"

Her brows drew together. "No, sir, just, 'You're the only one.' Then my baby cried and I never paid that man no more attention. Law, I never been so happy to hear him crying, that's the truth. I done thought he froze to death."

"He'll be safe now," Father reassured her even as he plucked at Mother's sleeve. "My dear, meet us out back in five minutes, no more. I'll take a lantern."

Mother slammed bureau drawers in the other room while Ibby held the baby. "Is this little one all you have?" She stroked his cheek as Mother bustled in with both hands full of stuff.

"All I have now. I pray I'll find my George in Canada. But I—" she faltered and dissolved in sudden tears. "My girl, her babies," she sobbed. "I left them." The raw grief was more than Johnny could bear.

"Johnny, you skedaddle, now." Mother's brisk command banished sentiment as she handed the woman a handkerchief. "We need to get these two into some dry clothes."

He slipped into his jacket and headed for the front door. "Will you call me before she goes?"

She gave him a distracted nod as she dragged the woman's dry shoes from under the stove. "Here's some socks for you, too, Auntie. My husband won't miss this one pair. They're good, warm wool."

Johnny left the house, plainly forgotten. Starlight showed the way to the fence. He leaned both elbows on the rail and propped up a foot. So he had seen a fugitive at last. He never hoped to hear a more thrilling story. He wondered exactly where the woman had crossed the ice.

The ice. He gripped the rail and frowned. He had heard the ice crack around midnight, yet the woman had crossed. That meant an ice bridge must remain. Hugh had chosen today, Thursday. Looked like Hugh had won, and Johnny was left out in the cold again.

Or was he? He squinted through the darkness toward the river, unable to believe his eyes. There was no ice bridge in sight now, just flashes of white as huge ice cakes tumbled and crashed toward the Mississippi. The Ohio was flowing again, as freely as it ever did in August. If the slave had crossed perhaps an hour later, she and her baby would have drowned.

He had no idea how long he stood there before Cutie whined and nosed his leg. She stretched to rest her paws on his side as she smiled and panted in his face. Then she cocked her head at a familiar jingle. The horses—the slave was leaving!

Johnny dashed around back with Cutie hot on his heels. He was wild to share the news about the ice, but everyone was busy. Father held the lantern high as Ibby rolled something up in her best apron, likely the woman's clothes. She tied the strings around it to make a pouch.

The stout woman wore one of Mother's brown linsey-woolsey dresses; she had barely knotted the ends of the belt. Mother carried the baby in a sling draped over her head and one shoulder; Johnny recognized his old curtains.

"It's warm here," Mother was saying, "but spring won't come for a good while yet in Canada, Auntie. Take my shawl." She clucked her tongue as she draped the heavy folds around the woman. "I don't know how you managed without one."

The woman stared down at herself in confused surprise. "Lawsy mercy!"

Johnny thought Father would keel over on the spot. "You don't mean to say you lost your shawl?"

Worry lined the slave's face. "My petticoat, too. I clean forgot 'til now. When that man jumped out at me—"

Father groaned. "We need to move. You boys take her a good long way from here. Try Gilliland's in Red Oak. Come home when you think it's safe. Here, Johnny, hold the lantern." He offered his arm to the old woman.

Father led her to a chair at the edge of the porch as David led Old Sorrel into the yard. Ibby looped the apron bundle over the pommel. After a couple of tries, the old woman stood on the chair. Father steadied her as she climbed aboard Old Sorrel's broad back. She hooked one knee around the awkward side-saddle. She hitched herself into place and reached for her baby, snug in the cream blanket and sling.

It seemed to Johnny that each family member had rehearsed his or her part in the escape. Cal swung up on his horse and led Old Sorrel. Father brushed away tears and clutched Mother's hand as they followed the horses to the fence. Mother waved good-bye without a worry in the world; nothing ever shook her faith. Ibby shivered and put an arm around Johnny. David lowered the fence and kissed his parents good-bye.

Old Sorrel tossed his head; even Johnny could see that he relished his work. Cal tugged on the reins and the tawny horse nickered. Old Sorrel moved so easy that he wouldn't have cracked an eggshell if he'd stepped on it, yet Johnny noticed that the woman twined her fingers through his flaxen mane. He wondered if she'd ever ridden before.

David coaxed his horse over the fence and raised the rail. Then he mounted and fell in behind Cal and the old woman.

"Lord bless you all." The slave's voice was husky. Tears flowed as she twisted in the saddle and gazed beyond the house, back toward Kentucky. What was she looking at? Johnny half-expected to see Zeke Means leap out of the darkness, but nobody was there. The faraway longing in the woman's eyes pierced his heart as she rode out of sight.

The excitement was over. Father retrieved the lantern and he, Mother, and Ibby trailed to the house. Johnny lagged behind them to lean against a post. How did his family manage? It had been well over ten years since the first fugitive had come through their house. No wonder Lowry had chosen to go to Lane Seminary. He was back in Cincinnati now, far away from Ripley and the demands of the Underground.

Cutie whined and nudged Johnny's hand. He patted her good night and opened the kitchen door. Mother and Ibby had already gone to bed. How anyone could sleep after hearing about the escape over the ice was more than he could figure. Johnny's heart pounded when he thought about the story.

He looked around. All the life had gone out of the house now that the slave was gone. Her story was shattering, yet he could barely remember what she looked like. Even the floor was dry and clean, without a speck of mud to mark her passage. For Johnny, everything had changed, but he had no way to prove it. He scowled. *I can't tell a soul anyway, so what does it matter?*

He jammed his hands in his pockets and padded to the front of the house. Ah! At least Father was still awake. There he sat at his desk, head bowed—no doubt praying for the slave woman and her baby. Johnny eased into the rocking chair. Here was one small difference, after all. When was the last time he'd been alone with Father? He barely rocked while Father prayed.

At length, Father wiped his eyes and donned his spectacles. "I hope she gets away," he murmured. He uncorked the ink bottle and took the goose feather quill from the scrolled rack on the ink stand. The plume twirled as he rolled the pen between his finger and thumb. Once, twice he dipped the nib and blotted it thoughtfully on the pen wiper. Then he hunched over his desk. The pen scratched as his fine script filled the paper.

Curiosity got the better of Johnny; he stole from his chair and sidled next to Father. "What are you writing?"

Father jerked and an ink blot spread spider legs on a corner of the page. "Johnny! I thought you'd gone back to bed. Is something wrong?"

He started to speak, but checked himself. Father would never understand how Johnny longed to spread the news of the slave's escape. He'd only get in trouble. He shrugged.

"I know," Father patted his arm. "Now that you've seen a fugitive, you know what slavery really is."

"I guess so." He shoved another log in the stove and watched it kindle.

"It's an atrocity. How could such a thing happen to a good Christian woman? For I firmly believe that the next time I see her, we shall both be in heaven."

"Are you writing about her?" Johnny edged closer. "About the slave?"

"She's a slave no longer." Father's chin jutted. "I'm writing a pamphlet. It's a cruel institution indeed that sells a woman and child like beasts of the field. I hope to make the church see what a crime that is."

Johnny dropped his jaw. Cautious Father intended to tell the slave's story. "Oh, Father! Let me help. We can tell how she crossed the ice with her baby." He rubbed his hands together. "When people know what she did to get away, nobody will keep slaves anymore."

"Hold on, Johnny!" Father rumbled like thunder. "No one can ever know about her. I will describe her plight in the vaguest terms, certainly not so anyone would recognize her. If you tell anyone, *anyone*, what happened tonight, her life and her baby's will be in grave danger."

Their cozy camaraderie vanished like smoke. "B-but I thought . . ."

"Think about the risk we take. The law says that if we are caught so much as *assisting* a slave to escape, I'll be fined one thousand dollars. That's more than I earn in three years, son."

"If that's the law . . ."

Father reached for his Bible. "It isn't God's law." He thumbed the limp pages. "The twenty-third of Deuteronomy, verse fifteen: 'Thou shalt not deliver unto his master the servant which is escaped from his master unto thee.' Our instructions could not be clearer, yet we are at the mercy of man's foolish law every time we aid a fugitive."

"But they've never caught us." He knew it was the wrong thing to say the minute the words left his mouth. He studied a smudge on his boot.

"No, by the grace of God, they haven't, but that doesn't mean nobody suspects us. Laban Biggerman does. He told Lowry so, last fall—and Johnny?" Father waited until Johnny met his eyes. "Biggerman has no conscience. That man . . ." He broke off. "That man has shaved Elijah's mane and tail more than once, solely because he's *my* horse. He buys and sells men, women, and children, and the good Lord knows how he abuses them. Biggerman won't depend on a judge to find me guilty if he ever catches us 'stealing slaves,' as he calls it. And he won't claim the reward on my head, either. He'll pull the trigger."

Johnny swallowed. A sick feeling settled into the pit of his stomach. Father's eyes penetrated right into his soul. He knew Father expected him to promise he would never tell anyone about the slave and the ice. He opened his mouth. "Maybe this time—"

"No, son." Father rubbed his forehead. When he spoke again, Johnny believed for a moment that all was forgotten. "How would you like to visit Lowry in Cincinnati? You could take some high school courses at Lane, maybe room with some of the other boys your age."

It sounded like a suggestion, but Johnny's heart sank when he understood what Father really meant. Until he could learn to control his tongue, his family couldn't afford to keep him around. He would be sent away from Ripley as soon as it could be arranged.

Chapter 6

ELIZA

ELIZA'S LEGS TINGLED with pins and needles. She could feel a raw place where the back of the saddle rubbed against her, and the sling that supported Mose dug into her neck. His whimpers would soon work up to a full squall.

The big boy ahead of her . . . Cal, was that his name? He sure kept his horse moving, and he chirruped to encourage her horse every few seconds. She'd lost track of how many creeks they'd crossed, but it had been a good half hour since they'd last bogged down in the mud. How in the world did these boys see in the dark? They must have eyes like hawks.

Riding horseback was pure comfort compared to walking, though. *My legs would've give clean out if I'd a-had to walk all this way. Angels, that's what these boys are.*

Every muscle in her body ached when Cal finally drew rein. She saw a clearing ahead and glimpsed the outline of a church building in the dim moonlight.

The party rode three abreast into the clearing just as Mose let out a wail to beat the band. A light flared in a window of the house and somebody hustled toward them with a lantern.

"Who be you?"

"It's David and Cal Rankin, Pastor Gilliland. We have business for you."

A timid-seeming man stopped at Eliza's side, his white hair

bright in the lantern light. He was dressed in an old black suit. "Is that a baby I hear?"

"Yes, sir."

"Lord love you! I'll fetch Mrs. Gilliland."

The two boys dismounted and stretched. Eliza peeled the smothery sling away from Mose. *Lawsy mercy, that boy is mad.* He squirmed and struggled to draw breath for another mighty howl.

"Give him here, deary." Eliza saw a merry face beneath a frilled cap. Mrs. Gilliland snuggled Mose as he hiccupped and sobbed. "Well, bless your heart, child. Did you come all this way with your mammy? Fetch that upping block here, David. She's about done in."

The three men helped Eliza slide down from Old Sorrel's broad back. Try as she might, she couldn't make her legs behave properly. She wobbled into the house, and it was all she could do to sit on the bed. Mrs. Gilliland laid Mose in her arms and removed Eliza's shoes.

"Can you manage to feed him, Auntie? I'll be back in two shakes of a lamb's tail."

Eliza nodded and leaned against the headboard. Her head drooped—had she dozed off? She blinked. Mrs. Gilliland had Mose again.

"My, aren't you the bright-eyed boy now, all ready for a bath." She crooned at the baby and pushed a flannel nightgown into Eliza's hands. "Shuck out of your things and I'll scrub them. You're about my size; put this on. Will you eat?"

Eliza shook her head. The first shaft of morning sunlight cheered the room as she turned her back to change. The flannel nightgown was so comfortable, she could barely prop her eyes open. She lumbered like an old bear onto the feather tick bed and slept.

Darkness had fallen again when she awoke. Where was she? She rolled over. There was no answering rustle from the corn shuck mattress she slept on every night. A sudden laugh startled her; she didn't recognize the voice. She groped for Mose's cradle, but her hand met only air.

Eliza sprang to her feet in alarm and doubled over in pain. Her arms and legs throbbed. She rubbed her knee and winced; it was a mass of tender bruises—from the ice. The whole ordeal came back to her in an instant: sold, the ice, Zeke Means, Mr. Rankin, the long ride in the dark with the two Rankin boys and Mose. She flexed a stiff arm and groaned. Well, she would gladly bear an aching body if it meant being free.

Only . . . her body wasn't all that ached. A keen pain smote her heart. Beulah and her precious children were still back in Kentucky.

Candlelight flooded the room; Eliza dashed away fresh tears. "Well, I thought you were never going to wake up!" Mrs. Gilliland shouldered the door open. "This boy of yourn is a sight. I had a time keeping him happy today so you could sleep. Poor dear, you were tuckered out."

"How long . . . ?"

"Why, you've slept the day away! Do you feel like you could eat something now? I saved you a plate." She handed Eliza her dress, all fresh and clean if a bit damp, and an old petticoat stiff with knitted lace. "Here are your things. I washed what was in your apron bundle, too, and did up some baby things for you. It's chilly this evening; I'm warming Jean Rankin's shawl. That *is* her shawl, isn't it? And wasn't that her old dress you had on? She would give away her last possession to help a body." She nudged the door closed with her foot until it admitted only a sliver of light, enough so Eliza could see to dress.

She skinned into her undergarments, kicked the nightgown aside, and slipped her own faded dress over her head. She tiptoed to peek at Mose, snuggled in the woman's arms. He wiggled with delight and gave her a gummy grin.

Mrs. Gilliland chatted as she led the way to the kitchen. "Now, Pastor Gilliland is in an awful hurry to get you under way, deary, but I told him we'd trust the good Lord to take care of matters so you could rest. I want you to come out here and have a bite to eat, and you pay him no mind. Your journey will keep."

Steam curled from a plateful of fried chicken and green beans that had been simmered with bacon. Mrs. Gilliland cut a slice of dried apple pie and poured cold milk, too. Eliza darted an uneasy glance at Pastor Gilliland, but he made no sign to hurry her along.

"Frances has never met a soul she didn't want to mother." He smiled at his wife. "I'll tell the boys to wait a bit."

Eliza made quick work of the hot meal. When she picked up her plate and cup, Mrs. Gilliland stopped her. "Now, now, I'll see to that. Get your boy ready. What's his name? I clean forgot to ask last night."

"Mose."

"Short for Moses? A fine, strong handle." She tilted her head like a curious chickadee. "Now, Moses is a Bible name, did you know that?"

"Yessum. My missus read the Bible."

Mrs. Gilliland stared. "Read the Bible *to* you?"

"No, ma'am, to her girls, but I heard her say. . ." She studied on her words to get them right. "Moses told old Pharaoh to let God's people go."

"Yes, he did. Yes, he did." Wonder and respect lit Mrs. Gilliland's eyes. She gave Eliza's arm a quick squeeze, like they shared a secret.

"Ready now, Mother?" Pastor Gilliland whispered from just outside the door.

Mrs. Gilliland kissed Mose with a smack. "On our way, deary."

Eliza wouldn't have thought it possible to ride a horse again so soon, but she found a position that mostly spared her raw skin and sore muscles. Pastor Gilliland held a quiet conference with his sons and gave instructions on which station to use. His wife fussed over Mose before surrendering him to his mother.

Eliza's heart overflowed at their matter-of-fact aid, offered like she was family. What words could make these kind people understand her gratitude? "God bless you," was all she said, but judging by the peaceful expressions on the Gillilands' faces as she rode away, it was enough.

The first five nights of April passed in a haze. Every time Eliza glanced ahead, she saw a horse's rump. It seemed like she had spent her entire life perched on a horse by night and asleep by day—by now, she probably even smelled like a horse. Her muscles tolerated the strange posture that the sidesaddle forced, but she paid dearly for the adjustment when she awoke and started off the next evening. Then she braced herself for a slow slog through deep mud to cover another ten miles or so northward on the way to freedom.

Always she sought pleasant thoughts to ward off her physical discomfort. Doggedly she called to mind George's dear face, his laugh, and his silly pranks. She had prayed so often that the Lord would protect and provide for her husband that it was easy to imagine the house that he lived in, with some good-hearted Canadian soul keeping watch until Eliza arrived to take over. She did not allow herself to think about Beulah and her family.

Patches of snow widened as the travelers left spring weather behind; if it was this cold here, Eliza dreaded to think what spring would be like in Canada. She drew Mrs. Rankin's shawl close to protect herself and Mose from the new bite in the wind.

What good hearts these people had! She had not known there were so many generous folks in the world, folks who would share all they had, who would even risk their lives so she and Mose could be free. *What makes them do it, Lord?*

"We're here." The man on the horse ahead of Eliza's reined aside and led her horse abreast. "Wonder if Doc Norton's about? I don't see a light."

"Maybe somebody's took sick." His partner nudged his horse forward just as a tall man with a leather bag approached them on foot.

"What's this? More business for me?"

"Yes, sir, Doc Norton. Got a baby with her, too."

"Goodness! Then I'm thankful that Mrs. Hall had her baby quickly." The doctor cracked a tired smile at the conductors. "I'm afraid it was a boy."

Eliza heard a snicker. "Well, the world can always use another Greenleaf Norton, eh, doc? Greenleaf Norton Hall. Sounds like a castle!"

Had she heard his name right? "Greenleaf" reminded Eliza of the doctoring herbs and seeds she carried in her kerchief to plant in Canada.

The doctor sighed. "Poor child. It's quite a mouthful, isn't it?" He led Eliza's horse toward the barn. "I don't know why ladies feel obliged to name their sons after the attending physician, but you may be sure of this: after my Amanda and I marry next month and start a family, there will be no Greenleaf Norton Junior if we are blessed with a boy." He reached up to Eliza. "Give me your baby and take my hand. Step right on that fence rail and hop down, Auntie, if you can manage it."

Eliza alighted with a thump that scattered the prowling barn cats. While she tidied her skirts, the doctor flipped back Mose's coverlet. He offered a delicate finger for Mose to hold; his skin was almost blue-white next to her baby's coffee-colored hand.

"What might your little one's name be? Not Greenleaf Norton, I'm sure."

"His name is Mose." This fine-looking doctor talked more than any of the men she'd met so far. In sharp contrast to meek Pastor Gilliland's garb, Dr. Norton wore a straw top hat and a houndstooth morning coat. She wondered how in the world he had kept his linen trousers spotless in all this mud.

One of the men gave a polite cough. "You need us for anything else, Doc?"

The doctor blinked. "Sorry, McCoy, you can head on home. Greet your folks for me." He might be very young, Eliza thought, but he was bone-tired.

McCoy winked. "God bless you on your journey, Auntie. Don't let the doc talk your leg off. He doesn't have a wife around to converse with, but all that will change soon!"

Doctor Norton chuckled. "See you boys later." He pointed to a tiny log cabin some distance away. "Welcome to Greenleaf's of Greenfield! Entirely too many Greens, that's what I say. Do you have any family besides Mose? I'm all alone here, you know."

Eliza's bundle twirled and bumped against her leg as she followed the man. "I ain't seen my husband since the fall." She gritted her teeth to keep from mentioning Beulah.

"I'm sorry."

Perhaps it was only a simple display of courtesy, but the doctor's civility hit Eliza hard. She caught her breath and wiped away a quick tear. "I been praying to God that I can find George when I gets to Canada."

"George is his name, eh?"

Eliza nodded. *The doctor is mighty stuck on names. No wonder, with a name like Greenfield.* "I sent him on ahead of me before winter come. Lawsy mercy, it's a good thing I did! I never seen the beat of the ice and snow we had."

"Yes, it was a bad winter. The snow's not all melted here yet. It played havoc with business, too."

She skirted a patch of crusty, white slush. "The doctorin' business, you mean? Now, that's a mighty fine thing for a man to do, take care of people for the good Lord."

"Well, yes, the snow did make it difficult to reach my patients, but what I meant was . . ." He peered into the deep woods that surrounded his cabin before whispering, ". . . *the Underground.*"

Eliza caught her breath. How many like her had he helped? Her heart overflowed with gratitude for his double sacrifice. "I bless God that He raised up men like you and Pastor Rankin to help me and Mose, and my George before us." Eliza puffed as she picked her way around a stretch of mud puddles. "Big strong man like my George, don't figure such a one as him to need much help, but he's feebleminded, and I—"

The doctor stopped in his tracks so suddenly that she almost bumped into him. "He's *what*?" His arms tightened around Mose, who whimpered.

"Yessir, feebleminded is what he is. Old master, he thumped George over the head with a hoe when he was barely man-grown, right after we was married. Made a big hollowed-out place on the back of his head, right here." Eliza reached to touch the same place on her own head, but her hand dropped back to her side. The most peculiar expression had settled over the doctor's features.

"'Feebleminded?'" He frowned. "What do you mean?"

"Wel-l-l," she hesitated. She wondered if she'd used the wrong doctoring word. "Well, ain't nothing wrong with his muscles. I reckon he can pick up most anything; he's that strong. But he won't hardly do nothin' 'less *I* tell him to. He's not right in the head no more; can't remember nothin' from one minute to the next. He fools around and cuts a shine most all the time, and law, he loves to eat! Only now," she confided, "everything tastes the same. Don't matter to George if an egg's spoiled rotten. I gots to watch him or he'll eat it. He can't smell nothin', neither."

"How extraordinary!" the doctor exclaimed. "I wonder . . ."

A warm glow wrapped around Eliza's heart. The more she talked about George, the closer he seemed. "Got a powerful deep voice, too. When he gets mixed up, he hollers my name, loud as can be." She grinned. "Reckon I could just about hear him now, clear from Canada."

Doctor Norton's bag slipped from his fingers and landed with a clank. His face was whiter than a hen's egg.

"What's wrong?" Eliza took her son from him without waiting for an answer. The man looked like a feather would knock him over.

"Only one word, all these months," the doctor muttered. He searched her face. "What's your name, Auntie?" He held up a hand. "No, don't tell me; mayhap I can guess it. By any chance"—the doctor's eyes glittered like feverish stars—"is your name Eliza?"

Every hair at the nape of her neck rose to attention. "How you know that?" she whispered.

"Bless you, I should know it well enough—he's said it hundreds of times!"

Her glance roamed the yard. "Who said it?"

"Why, George, of course! It *must* be him. It's just—think of the hand of God, that you should be reunited at my house. He's here." He trembled and laughed, a sharp bark like a fox.

He's touched in the head, too, Eliza thought wildly. She backed away and spoke slowly, like she always did to George. "My man's in Canada, long time gone." She bobbed her head to soothe the doctor while she edged toward the woods. "You's just tired, that's what. You been busy with a new baby. Go on up and get some rest. Me and this boy'll stay in the barn."

"Stay in the barn, when your husband's in my house?" He laughed again and reached for her arm. "Certainly not. I'd like to see you try it!"

From the corner of her eye, Eliza watched a rooster stretch its scrawny neck. Its dusty wings flap, flap, flapped. She knew what was coming. Sure enough, the rooster's jubilant crow exploded at the doctor's boot heels. He flinched and shielded his ears.

In that instant, one thought flashed into Eliza's mind—*run*. She clutched Mose to her chest, spun away from the doctor's grasp, and crashed into the thicket at the forest's edge. Briars snagged the shawl; she shrugged out of it. A branch lashed her forehead. She hiked her skirts high and sprinted headlong into the woods.

Too soon, Mose's small weight sapped her strength. She ran only a few rods before her legs gave out. She dodged behind fallen timber, flopped to the ground, and clapped a hand over Mose's mouth.

Her breath rasped in her throat and hot tears trickled. Why had she trusted white men? Well, no more. She and Mose would journey to Canada alone—if she could get away from this crazy man.

"Eliza!"

Her heart pounded. Could the doctor see her? He sounded very near. Cold crept up through her dress and she shook all over.

"Eliza!"

Closer yet. She rose to a crouch behind the huge, mossy log, poised to run. Something scampered over her foot and scrambled to perch atop the log; a field mouse watched her with shoe-button eyes.

"Oh, what have I done?" the doctor moaned. "I didn't mean to alarm you."

She heard his boots, no, *two* pairs of boots, scuff through brittle leaves—the doctor was not alone, after all.

"Please come out! The heavy snow made it impossible to send your George to Canada; you must believe me. He was seriously ill, besides." The boots scuffed again and stopped. "It was pleurisy. It took him ever so long to recover."

His words sounded like the truth. How she wanted to believe the man! But she had Mose to think of—she must not risk it.

The doctor said something almost too low to catch: "You say it."

Seconds stretched out so long and silent that the field mouse dozed. The next instant the mouse bolted when someone bellowed, *"Eliza!"*

The deep voice splintered a chill to the base of her spine. Cold fire spread to her core. She must not stand up, she *must not*, but she was on her feet already.

She looked everywhere at once until she honed in on two indistinct shapes. The doctor's white trousers gleamed in the early morning light that outlined the edge of the forest. Beside the doctor stood a tall, thin scarecrow of a man. Eliza squinted; her knees buckled. She whispered, "George."

The thin man broke through the thorns and barreled toward her. He hurtled over the massive log like it was a twig. Then George lifted Eliza and Mose clean off the ground and held on for dear life. "I love you," he said.

Eliza wept with relief—and joy. Mose bawled until the doctor gently dislodged him from between his parents. "Thank you, thank you, thank you," she breathed.

Twice the physician attempted to answer. At last, he only smiled at Eliza through his tears.

Chapter 7

Johnny

THE LONGER HE THOUGHT about Father's decision to send him away, the better Johnny liked the idea. The great day finally came; he boarded the steamer on his own. His troubles melted like the winter's ice as he left Ripley behind.

When Johnny arrived in Cincinnati, Lowry met him at the dock as arranged. But then he engaged a stagecoach bound for the Beechers' home in Walnut Hills and sent Johnny on alone. Lowry had some pressing business downtown and warned Johnny that he might not be home before the next morning. Consequently, Johnny had no chance to ask Lowry about the famous Beechers, whose every action was news.

Well, he would meet the family on his own. How fortunate that he was not diffident, like Lowry. He never had the least bit of trouble making new friends. Johnny relished the chance to form his own impressions of a normal Christian family, as opposed to his own.

"Thanks!" Johnny hopped out of the stagecoach and retrieved a small trunk from the driver. The man touched his cap and whistled up his team. The stage lurched away and left Johnny standing alone outside a pretty house on Gilbert Avenue. Beech trees crowded the grounds of the place where he would stay for the next three months. Cincinnati! A thousand possibilities awaited him here, and he intended to explore every one of them.

The front of the house looked shut up and deserted. Country manners directed him to call at the back door, where inviting porches wrapped around the two wings of the house on both stories.

The sky darkened and Johnny glanced up. "Oh, no," he muttered. He hoisted the trunk over his head and headed for the shelter of the porch. Before he reached the steps, a multitude of passenger pigeons flew above him. Their flight was far swifter than the fastest horse could gallop, and they flew so close together that they blotted out the wan April sunlight. The birds alighted in the stately beeches until Johnny could not see the trees themselves. Still, the flock increased. Feathered bodies stacked up like blocks, rosy breast on blue back. Dead branches snapped beneath the sheer weight. There was ample evidence that the birds had roosted here before, which was why Johnny prudently ducked under his trunk.

The back door banged against the bricks and rattled on its hinges. A gray-haired man stormed out on the porch and shoved his spectacles to rest on top of his head, right in front of another pair. He hefted an ancient fowling piece. "Pigeons!" he screamed.

Johnny didn't hesitate; he pitched the trunk and dropped flat to the ground. His heart hammered. With one cheek pressed in the mud, he eyed the man with the gun.

The man may have been elderly, but he was spry. He leveled the firearm at his hip and let the charge fly in a flash of powder and smoke. Buckshot whistled toward a beech tree near the barn. There was a fluttery squawk, a partial exodus, and a hail of dead birds. Johnny heard the *snick* of the flintlock and a second report. More birds plumped to earth.

"Got 'em!"

Slowly, Johnny raised his head. The man propped his gun against the house and braced both hands on the porch rail. He vaulted to the ground and trotted to the foot of the tree. His lips moved as he pointed at the pile of pigeons. "Say, Charles!" he shouted, "I got thirty-three that time!"

"Yes, Father, but you've frightened our guest out of a year's growth, as well." A stoop-shouldered young man descended the porch steps and crossed to offer Johnny a hand. "I have shirts that are not so white as his complexion."

Johnny brushed dead leaves from his jacket and wiped mud from his cheek with shaky hands. "I'm all right."

The older man's generous mouth split his face in a proud grin. "Well, well, where did you spring from? Did you see that shot?"

"You may be sure he did, sir." The young man's expression was droll, but his eyes were kind. "Father is quite harmless. Are you Johnny Rankin? I'm Charles Beecher, and this is Dr. Beecher."

Johnny stared in wonder as the president of Lane Seminary nodded with comical dignity. "Oh, bless my soul, you're John Rankin's son? Come along, my boy! Let me take your things. Lyddie! Company's here!" Dr. Beecher wrested the trunk from the mud, skipped up the steps, and sailed into the house.

Charles sighed. "What must we Beechers look like to an outsider? I've often wondered. But your face speaks volumes, and not with words that flatter us, I fear." He directed Johnny through the house to the parlor and pottered off to find his father.

In the parlor, a fire blazed on the massive hearth. Heaped on the sofa was a pile of shot, ready for the next flock of pigeons. Johnny's trunk was plopped in the middle of a braided rug, presumably where Mr. Beecher had dropped it. Johnny shook his head and removed his hat. A lady entered the room. Her gracious smile calmed him. She looked much younger than Johnny's mother; he supposed she must be Charles's wife.

"Welcome, Johnny! So you've come from Ripley!" She rang a bell and kept talking. "My, my, all that way by yourself. Sadie, please take this young man's things to the first guestroom at the back of the house."

"Yassum." The colored woman steamed up the steps like a barge.

"Have you had your dinner?" His hostess was on the verge of ringing the bell again.

"Yes, ma'am, Mrs. Beecher, thank you."

"Came all by yourself, my, my. You're awful young, aren't you?"

Johnny fidgeted. Yes, all by himself, and he had relished every moment of independence. Each mile had put Ripley and the secret Underground farther behind. "I'm twelve."

"Well, come up and get settled in your room."

When he looked in the doorway, he saw a cluster of beech trees just outside the tall window. There were no leaves yet, but hundreds of roosting pigeons blocked what little light filtered through. Against one wall was a double bed with a nine-patch quilt and a plump pillow. "Who do I share the bed with?" he asked.

"What? Oh, nobody. Now, Joe and Tom are just across the hall in their room if you need anything. Would you excuse me, please? I'll be back to check on you later." Her green-barred skirts swished as she hurried down the hall.

The room was perhaps a quarter the size of the long room that Johnny shared with his five brothers back home, but it was all his. Now he understood Lowry's gloating about having his own bed when he went away to Lane.

The breeze coaxed a mournful whistle from the ill-fitted window, and Johnny heard a scratch. A branch tip covered with tight buds skritched against the porch rail.

His room was powerful warm. For the first time, he noticed the fire laid in a small fireplace; he must be above the blaze downstairs, too. He raised the sash of his window and leaned out to cool off.

Snickers erupted from beneath the window. Johnny looked down to see two boys squatting on the upper porch. They stared up at him with frank interest.

"Hello," said one of the boys. He brushed back a hank of auburn hair. Light blue eyes sparkled and belied his bland expression. "The wind spoiled our surprise."

"Hi," Johnny answered, instantly on guard. He stood back to let the boys climb in the window.

"My name's Tom," the auburn-haired boy said. He had slim shoulders and a narrow waist, and he stood a head taller than Johnny. He jerked a thumb toward the other boy. "This is Joe Jackson. Where'd Magpie get to, Joe?" he asked. Joe shrugged; Johnny decided it could not have been Joe's idea to hide. Tom went on, "Ah, well, you'll meet his sister Magpie later." At a reproachful glance from Joe, he corrected, "Sorry, you'll meet *Maggie* later."

"I'm Johnny Rankin."

"Saw you arrive. We came out when we heard the twenty-one gun salute." Tom flopped to his stomach on the bed and waved his heels in the air.

Johnny relaxed. Tom was full of fun, but he also had a wistful air that was appealing. He and Johnny would certainly be good friends, and it appeared that whatever Tom did, Joe followed.

Two friends already, and he'd barely been in Cincinnati an hour. He unpacked the trunk while Tom chattered about high school. A current seminary student, Mr. Patterson, was the teacher; he taught to earn his tuition.

"He's a good fellow," Tom assured Johnny.

"What time do classes take up?" Johnny arranged a shirt in the wardrobe. "I forgot to ask your mother."

Tom's eyes dulled. "My stepmother, you mean. My mother passed away almost three years ago."

"You saw *my* mother," Joe supplied. This boy could not sit

still, Johnny noted. He bounced his seat on the bed and clapped his hands together before each new bounce.

"Stop that, Joe," Tom said dutifully. "Father married Joe and Maggie's mother in Boston. She's very kind and loving." *But she's not my mother.* Tom's unspoken words filled the room with longing.

Johnny sought to comfort his new friend. "At least you still have your father . . . and your grandfather."

"My grandfather?" Tom's heels stilled and he quirked an eyebrow.

"The one with the gun."

Tom chuckled. "He's a grandfather, all right, but he's not mine. He's my father, Dr. Lyman Beecher. Joe's mother is his third wife."

"Your father?" Johnny gaped.

"Yep," Tom said. "It's hard to keep everyone straight. Don't worry about the six eldest Beechers—some of them *I* haven't even met but once. They're mostly grown up and gone, but Harriet's here—she married Professor Stowe." Joe snickered, but Tom paid him no mind. "You met Charles, my half-brother, out front. James is my full brother, younger than me; you'll meet him. Bell's my only real sister. She doesn't live here, though." Tom pressed his lips together. "I write to her a lot."

Joe piped up between bounces. "Who's died in your family?"

Tom snorted in disgust and shoved his stepbrother. Joe sprawled to the floor and rubbed his elbow. "That's not good manners, Joe. You'll make him sad."

"Oh, no, it's all right," Johnny hurried to reassure them. "No one's died except Grandfather Lowry, and he was pretty old." He closed his trunk and shoved it under the bed.

"No one else?" Tom and Joe stared at Johnny as if he'd sprouted another head. "How many are in your family?"

Johnny paused to count. "Thirteen children and my mother and father." He sensed it would be folly to add the aunts, uncles, and cousins who stayed with them occasionally.

"But what about cholera?" Joe forced out the dreaded word.

"It was bad a couple of years ago. Four people a day died in Ripley. My mother, father, and my brother Lowry helped take care of them all."

"But nobody in your family died?" Tom looked dazed. He got up abruptly and took the clock from the mantel. He checked the time, wound the clock, and set it ticking again.

"No, but Mandy—" Johnny stumbled over her name. He reached in his pocket like he always did when he was nervous. Mandy was forever losing hair ribbons; they slid right out of her hair. He looped one he'd kept between two fingers and felt the comforting squeak under his thumb. "Mandy, who my brother is going to marry, her father passed away, and her little brother almost died."

When Tom finally spoke again, Johnny was surprised at the bitterness in his voice. "They told Father before we moved to Walnut Hills that it was so healthy here that we would have to leave to get sick. Yet there is no one in this house who has not lost a family member since we came." He looked out the window and sighed. "I'm sorry. It's nothing to do with you." Tom offered his hand to Johnny, who shook it. "School starts at nine tomorrow morning. We walk over with Charles and James. Sometimes Magpie walks with us; you can, too."

So began the pattern of Johnny's days at Lane Seminary. Each morning, the Beecher boys escorted him over the wooded path to the school. Charles sang a different hymn every day. He showed great pleasure when Johnny sang in tune; he made him keep the melody from then on while he sang harmony. Johnny reflected that even after years in the church choir, he had never heard so fine a voice as Charles had. "Good and loud" was the best he could say for Tom's singing, and Joe often just listened. When Charles coaxed James to join in, too, his little-boy treble was so pure that sometimes it brought tears to Charles's eyes. Johnny grew to love the morning walks to school.

Mr. Patterson was a fair teacher, who rightly judged that Johnny would never be a speller. Johnny had decided a long time ago that though he talked like Father, he wrote like Mother, a very inventive speller. Sometimes he caught Mr. Patterson hiding a smile as he read Johnny's work. He hoped Mr. Patterson didn't tell Lowry; the two young men were good friends.

The grounds of Lane Seminary were beautiful. Johnny's classes met in the chapel, but the building was far finer than the simple name implied. Six Doric columns marched across the portico; it looked like a Grecian temple. When the chapel bell rang, Johnny scaled the steps with the other boys and entered through doors flung open wide to allow the air to circulate. There was no shoe scraper to bother with as there was at Father's church. The halls and lecture room floors were almost as covered with mud as the barn floor back home, but the library above the chapel was a bit neater. Professor Stowe had personally amassed more than ten thousand volumes from England and Europe to make Lane's the largest library west of the Allegheny Mountains. There was space for thirty thousand volumes, but Johnny could hardly imagine so many books in one place.

The dormitory where Lowry lived was a four-story building, a hundred feet long by forty feet wide. There were rooms for eighty-four students, and there was a basement—where Lowry had made brooms, he proudly told Johnny as he gave him a tour. Lowry was so busy with his studies and whatever business took him so often into Cincinnati that Johnny rarely saw his brother, but there were plenty of other people to fill his free time.

He met farm boys like himself at Lane, but he met the sons of professors, too. Professor Biggs's son, Henry, was a willing comrade in his adventures, and so was Sam Broadwell. Professor Biggs had taken Sam in when his wealthy father died. Sam's mother was an invalid and was not able to care for him. Sam was younger than the other fellows and smart as a whip. Yet Johnny could see the same sadness in Sam's eyes that marked Tom's expression. He chalked it up to another family torn asunder.

Sometimes, Tom entertained the boys with legends of his famous half-brother, Henry Ward Beecher, and his past exploits at Lane. Henry Ward had roomed with Professor Stowe in the other building on campus, where the teachers lived. "Professor Stowe had a terrible time waking Henry, so one day he just gave up. After he stomped off to morning prayers, Henry sprang out of bed and threw on his clothes—he always did dress like a ragbag, anyhow," Tom laughed. "His friends said he had a place for everything, and that place was on the table. At any rate, he dressed and shot through the woods like a deer. When Professor Stowe arrived, there was Henry Ward in his seat, hands folded and his head bowed."

Johnny laughed with the other boys, but he marveled at Tom's cool demeanor. Tom was leaving tomorrow for Marietta College in southeastern Ohio, despite his best efforts to persuade Dr. Beecher to let him stay at Lane. For Tom, there would be no more trips to the swimming hole in the creek, no more wild games of follow-the-leader, no more trees to climb. His stoicism saddened Johnny, but the boys had planned one last glorious game of hide-and-seek in their friend's honor. Johnny smirked to himself; he'd spied out the perfect hiding place.

After a supper of fresh white bread spread with home-churned butter and blackberry jam, the boys met at twilight by the barn. Johnny munched on an apple while they waited for Henry and Sam to arrive.

"Last one to the barn is it!" he heard. He wiped his mouth on his sleeve and dashed to tag up. Joe was last to touch, so he accepted his fate and leaned against the side of the barn to count to one hundred while the other boys scattered in glee.

Johnny skinned up the beech tree at the back corner of the house. All the boys said this tree was unclimbable, but they didn't know they were talking to the Ripley tree-climbing champion. Johnny's self-congratulations ended when he discovered what they meant. He had forgotten that this tree had lately been used as a pigeon roost. Pigeon droppings dotted the tree branches. He avoided the worst mess as he climbed toward the upstairs verandah.

Now for the dicey part of his plan. The branch that scraped the verandah railing whenever the wind blew looked a lot skinnier than it had from his window; it was slippery, too. Could he make it across? He stood up and gripped the branch above him; he hoped he was invisible in his dark clothes.

Every time his hand met a pigeon deposit, he grimaced, but at last he gripped the roof and swung noiselessly down to the verandah. He spread-eagled himself on the boards and scooted on his stomach beneath his window at the corner. At last he reached the prized position, just short of the French doors that led to Dr. Beecher's study. He inched to the railings and peered through.

Just as he'd hoped, he could see everything below, but he doubted anyone could see him. Ah, he spied Henry, crouched behind the rain barrel. Over there, James and Sam stood two abreast behind a narrow tree, trusting in a small-boy way that because they could not see anyone, no one could see them. He watched Joe blunder about the log pile—it would be ages before he found somebody.

Johnny took out his handkerchief and cleaned his fingers and jacket, smelly but victorious. Wait a minute—where was Tom? He scanned the back yard again.

The back door creaked. "Papa? I'm here!" It must be Mrs. Stowe. Light illuminated the yard. Then Johnny saw Tom.

He was sitting in plain sight on a bench that encircled the biggest tree in the yard. Maggie Jackson, the only girl among all the resident boys, sat next to him. She stroked his back with a dainty hand. Tom hunched forward, oblivious to comfort, elbows on knees. He held his head in both hands. His shoulders quivered.

The yard went dark. Johnny felt as if he'd been sucker punched. All at once, he longed for Ripley, to see Mother and Father and all his brothers and sisters. Why would the Beechers send Tom away from his family when family was what he craved more than anything else in the world?

He heard footsteps in the study. Startled, he wondered whether Joe had spotted him. Johnny rolled against the wall and held his breath.

"Papa?" Mrs. Stowe said again. Johnny relaxed. He heard the davenport squeak. "Well, I guess he's gone, Lowry."

Johnny's eyes popped open. What was Lowry doing here?

"Thank you for walking over with me this evening. You really needn't have bothered. I know how busy you are with your studies . . . and everything."

"No trouble at all, Mrs. Stowe," Lowry said. "I promised the professor I'd watch out for you while he's away."

"Well, I am grateful. Please go back to your books. I'll wait here for Papa, and he'll make sure I get home, or one of the boys will take me."

Lowry's boot heels clicked to a stop. "Oh, Mrs. Stowe," he added nonchalantly, "I surely appreciate that you have kept my secret all these months. I've had a lot of business lately." He hesitated. "It helps that someone knows where I may be found, if I ever meet up with any . . . trouble."

If Johnny had been a dog, he could not have perked up his ears with more interest. What secret was Lowry talking about? Johnny was sure of one thing—it wasn't the Underground. Old rock-solid Lowry, with his taunts of "Go ask Johnny!" would never reveal *that* secret.

But Mrs. Stowe did not immediately relieve his curiosity. He imagined her homely face, with the prominent Beecher nose that looked so manly on her father's face but so out of place on her own. She was plain and quick as a drab Jenny wren. Her one great beauty was her luminous eyes. Sometimes it seemed as if he could see all of life itself in them. They practically glowed when she was lost in thought.

"Now, Lowry, we won't speak of that. You were out of your head with fever then, and we little noted what you said. We only prayed to God to make you well again."

Better and better, thought Johnny. What exactly had Lowry said?

"All ye, all ye outs in free!" Joe's yell reverberated. Johnny edged closer to the French doors to hear better.

A paper rustled. "What's this?" Mrs. Stowe asked.

"Father wrote this pamphlet. I thought you might like to see it."

"Oh . . . thank you." The slightest hint of a question lingered in her voice.

Lowry coughed. "When I was sick, you said you wanted to do something, to aid in something—the Underground."

Johnny clapped a hand to his mouth.

"Fancy your remembering that!" She sounded very pleased. Johnny heard another rustle. "It's very long, isn't it? What is it about?"

"Father wrote it this winter, to tell churches about the desperate lengths slaves go to when they want to escape."

"That's only natural, Lowry," she said with spirit.

"Yes, but . . . this slave was different." Boot heels clicked. Johnny pictured Lowry twirling his hat round and round by the brim, the sweat from his fingers dampening it. "She . . ."

The davenport squeaked again. *"She?"*

"I knew you would be interested, seeing you're a writer. She came through in March, just before the ice broke up, or rather, *as* the ice broke up."

"Lowry," she whispered his name in horror, "you don't mean to say the poor creature crossed the ice?"

"Yes." Relief warmed his brother's voice. Lowry was usually at his social best when he was about to take his leave. "That's exactly what I mean. It's not often that a woman her age escapes. She was a Christian, too, according to Father."

"Oh." Mrs. Stowe dragged the word out, and Johnny knew the dreamy look was on her face.

Apparently Lowry recognized that look, too. "Good-bye, Mrs. Stowe." Johnny heard the grate of the door handle. "I only wish Father had written about the baby."

The pamphlet fluttered. "What baby?" Mrs. Stowe demanded.

"Why, I . . ." Lowry trailed off in consternation. "The slave woman crossed the ice with her baby. Held the little fellow in a sling made of her petticoat, or shawl, or something."

"No. Oh, no." Johnny heard a quick intake of breath, almost a sob. "Why?"

"Sold down the river, to hard labor."

"A baby. They sold her baby?" Her shoes tapped a staccato rhythm. There was a rustle and a sharp exclamation from Lowry. "Tell me her story, Lowry. Please, tell me all about her."

"But, Mrs. Stowe," Lowry began miserably, "I didn't see her. I wasn't there, I'm sorry." Silence. Then, "Here, sit down." The davenport squeaked again. "You're all flustered. There, you'll feel better soon."

The boot heels beat a hasty retreat and the door clicked shut with a sharp finality. For a moment, silence reigned. Then the sobs came, great wracking sobs that must have shaken her whole body. Poor Mrs. Stowe! Johnny stood up and peeped through the glass as she buried her face on the back of the davenport and wept. His heart melted. Small wonder Mrs. Stowe mourned for the slave woman, whose heart's dearest desire had been to keep her family together in freedom.

Every detail of the slave's escape—the heavy child, the syca-more trees, the red shawl—crowded into his thoughts, as clear as the razor-thin ice that had jutted over the water that night.

The door handle gave under his hand before he knew what was happening. He knelt beside Mrs. Stowe and brushed her arm with a touch as light as a moth's wing. She turned, her beautiful eyes dulled with grief. What could he possibly say to comfort her?

"Lowry wasn't there that night, Mrs. Stowe." Johnny lifted his chin. "But I was."

Chapter 8

ELIZA

"MAMA, MAMA!" For the tenth time, Mose patted Eliza's face as she stared at the woman across the street. Surely to goodness, it was Aunt Kate, but Levi Coffin's happy home was far behind her now. All of wind-tossed Lake Erie lay between the Coffins and Eliza. Why would Aunt Kate be here in Canada West?

Levi and Catherine Coffin, dressed in their Quaker garb, had taken Eliza's family into their home in Newport, Indiana, just north of Richmond. By that time, Eliza had been worn to a frazzle with keeping Mose quiet while they traveled to freedom, to say nothing of George and his outbursts. Aunt Kate sized up the situation immediately—"Thee needeth rest!"—and took over, receiving Eliza and her family into their home for several weeks. One night, the Coffins had even hidden Eliza in their feather mattress when slave hunters searched their house.

Aunt Kate and Eliza had grown very close, but that was months ago—Eliza had only to listen to Mose's jabbering to know how time had flown. He'd spoken his first words in Canada, in freedom.

Eliza touched her tongue to the gap where Laban Biggerman had knocked out her tooth and thought for a minute. Likely the woman just looked familiar, she decided, but she had to know. She dodged buggies and wagon wheels and crossed the busy street. "Aunt Kate!"

Sure enough, the woman turned with an expectant smile. She searched the crowd and looked right through Eliza twice.

"Aunt Kate, it's me, Eliza! Lookahere how big Mose's got to be!" Eliza laughed and held him up for inspection.

Confusion puckered the woman's forehead. "Do I know thee?"

Eliza searched the Quaker woman's face beneath the familiar bonnet. No doubt about it—the gentle manner and sweet face belonged to Catherine Coffin.

"Why . . . you hid me in your mattress! George and me, we live with a minister here. I cook and keep house for Pastor Wilks, and I'm saving up my money . . ."

"Oh, yes?"

A stranger would have answered in the same offhand way, with casual attention paid to details that didn't matter. Hard as it was to believe, Aunt Kate had forgotten her. Maybe it was not so hard, after all—hadn't Uncle Levi said that thousands of fugitives had passed through their home? To them, Eliza was just one of a long line of forgotten faces and stories.

"Well, good-bye, Aunt Kate," she said. "God bless you."

"Fare-thee-well, child."

Eliza watched the familiar Quaker cloak pass sedately from her life. She kissed Mose and forced her steps along the boardwalk.

Pastor Wilks had patiently taught her that she must take her burdens to the Lord. She'd tried so hard to pray away her loneliness. The white folks in Canada West let her live in freedom, but they were not friendly. Other refugees were just as busy as Eliza was, trying to earn a living. The only people who really loved her in this world were her own family: George and Mose—and Beulah.

How old would Beulah's children be? She could barely remember their faces, try as she might. Beulah, now, her beauty was burned for eternity into Eliza's memory, but had the grandbabies forgotten their old Mammaw, too?

A tear trickled down Eliza's cheek. Mose saw it and laughed. He laid his head on her shoulder and she wrapped him tight in her arms. Well, she would storm heaven with her prayers until the Lord saw fit to answer. She didn't care how long it took.

Part 2
1841

Chapter 9

JOHNNY

JOHNNY LEANED ON HIS hoe and fanned the muggy air with his hat. The July sun blazed down on the garden, and it was useless to wish for a cool breeze or a chunk of ice. His stomach rumbled—he guessed it must be near noon.

He watched Cal and Sam mounding earth around the potato plants. Cutie lay across the path to the house. She poked her graying muzzle toward the north and tested the air. The old dog rolled to her feet and pricked her ears. Johnny watched her; she didn't bark. Instead, she sat down and tipped her head to scratch the white ruff around her neck. Johnny sighed and knocked down more weeds.

A few moments later, a movement north of the potato patch caught his eye. He squinted; two strangers, one white and one colored, walked through the cornfield toward the Rankin home.

The white man rolled his steps from heel to toe as he walked, but what Johnny noticed most was the picturesque way he was dressed. He wore a blue wool roundabout jacket that ended at his waist. Johnny had stopped wearing roundabouts about five years ago, when he was ten. This man wore curious trousers made of cotton duck, too, wider at the bottom. They flapped so high above his ankles that his lace-up Jefferson shoes showed. The crowning indignity in Johnny's eyes was that the man wore no suspenders to secure his trousers. Instead, they were fastened to his checkered shirt with two large cloth-covered buttons.

Johnny did not dare to look at his brothers for fear he would laugh out loud. He glanced at the other stranger.

This man was short, with a straw hat pulled low and a raggedy jacket stuffed to bursting. He stopped to stare across the wide river to the green Kentucky hills that shimmered in the haze.

Johnny shook his head; he had a funny feeling that this had all happened before. In any case, Father would know what to do about these men. Before he could holler to his father, the second man locked eyes with Johnny and grinned. Even at this distance, he could see there was something wrong with the stranger's teeth.

He spotted his parents over yonder, picking raspberries. The second stranger followed his gaze. When he saw Johnny's parents, he flashed another gap-toothed smile and altered his course to make a beeline for them.

Johnny heaved another sigh and turned back to his work, but a little voice nagged him that something did not add up. What was it? He turned back to search the stranger's face as he approached Mother and Father. My goodness, such a wide smile, wide and snaggle-toothed. Of *course*, the odd smile was caused by a missing tooth, one right in the front . . . and then his brain clicked. Johnny's hoe toppled to the ground. The second stranger was not a man at all—it was the slave woman who had crossed the frozen Ohio River with her baby. There could be no mistake.

But that was forever long ago. He searched his memory as the pair wended their way through the corn. Lowry and Mandy— had they been married a year yet? No, it would be a year this fall, and Ibby and her husband, John, would celebrate their first anniversary the day after. The double wedding was a good way to mark time, but the slave escape he was thinking of was surely longer ago than that.

Johnny turned from happy memories to something more

dangerous. How long ago had Jairus Shoup and Ben Mitchell attempted to search the house, with their snarling brindle bull-dogs in tow? Father had been preaching out of town that day, and Lowry had made his first trip into Ripley after recovering from another long illness.

Memory of the events flooded back like he was there again. It had been just before his fourteenth birthday, Johnny recalled, because Father had given him his own shotgun a few days later. Pity he hadn't given it sooner.

Johnny and Mother were waiting for Sam and Cal to return from Red Oak after they'd escorted a fugitive the night before. Shoup and Mitchell pounded on the door as the bulldogs choked against their collars. It went without saying that those two men were not smart enough to act on their own; they were Laban Biggerman's hired henchmen. Biggerman had been trying for a long time to catch the Rankins with "stolen" slaves under their roof. After the escape the previous night, he'd stepped up the pressure. He'd been crafty enough to instruct Shoup to ask about a white thief, not an escaped slave, but Mother called their bluff.

Johnny was shocked when Mother invited the men in to search the house. Maybe she figured the slave was long gone, and she was buying time for Cal and Sam to hide while she kept the men busy in the house. Whatever her reasoning, such a thing had never happened before, and Johnny knew it was wrong. He raced to get Father's shotgun and leveled it at the men.

"Halt! No slave hunter's coming in our house," he shouted. The men tried to calm Johnny down, but he stood his ground, and they left the porch.

Then reinforcements arrived, but for the wrong side. "Fan out, boys!" sang Ben Mitchell, the duller of the two men. In no time, the back yard was surrounded by men with guns, all determined to search the house. Johnny knew then that it was no accident that Father was out of town. This attack had been planned for a long time. One thing Biggerman hadn't counted on, though—the magistrate had declined to issue a search warrant, so the Kentuckians had no legal right to enter their house.

Johnny's knees were knocking by that time, but Mother remained perfectly calm. Then Sam motioned to them from behind the door. He'd skulked from the barn through the peach orchard and slipped in an open window unnoticed during all the commotion out back. Johnny was never so glad to see his brother.

Sam kicked the back door shut and took the gun from Johnny. Mother threw the bolt to lock the door and told Johnny to run out the front door and down the hill to town. He was to find Lowry and David and bring them home on the double. The bulldogs yammered and hurled themselves at the back door until it shuddered, but Johnny knew that if the dogs were out back, then it was safe to head out front and on to town.

Johnny hurdled the fence and tore down the hill even faster than he had tripped and rolled all those years ago. He told every friend he saw that John Rankin's house was under siege. When he finally tracked down Lowry, David, and Uncle William, they sped to Mother's aid and left Johnny far behind. By the time Johnny reached the hilltop, Lowry stood at the front door like grim death, holding Shoup and Mitchell at bay. Johnny hid behind his hedge apple tree and waited to see what would happen.

Then Biggerman himself arrived with seven more men. The slave trader ambled up the hill, slouch hat pushed back. The man closest to Biggerman commanded the most attention. He hefted a Bowie knife with a blade fifteen inches long.

The Rankins watched Biggerman swagger to within ten feet of the house. Lowry leaned against the front door and offered a solemn warning. "Don't come any nearer."

The slave trader curled his lip. "Ben Mitchell told me he found my slave's tracks in your yard. I'm going in." His foot touched the step.

Somebody would have died then, most likely Lowry himself, if he hadn't braced his back against the door and shoved Biggerman away with his foot. Biggerman staggered backward and missed the Bowie knife by inches.

"Say the word, Lowry, and I will break every bone in his slave-hunting body in less than a minute!" Jolly Bob Patton passed Biggerman to take his place beside Lowry on the step. The huge man pointed, and Johnny peeked around the tree to see at least a hundred friends, neighbors, and family members filing through the gate to surround the slave hunters.

Johnny grinned. That was when a good story got even better. Someone hollered, "Ben Mitchell! Where is Ben Mitchell?"

It was Cal.

Mitchell cried out, "Here!"

"I found some tracks! Come tell us if these are the slave's!"

Jairus Shoup held both of the brindled bulldogs and gave a huge grin. "Let's go, Ben!" Ben's chest swelled with pride as he swaggered over to Cal.

A knot of friends surrounded Cal at the point of the hill. Johnny shouldered his way through to stand beside his brother.

Cal pointed at a small patch of damp earth. "Do you recognize these?" Two footprints showed plainly, toes dug in as though the maker had been running hard.

It was a triumphant moment for Ben. "Them's the slave's very tracks, sure enough!"

"You all are my witnesses." Cal grew solemn. "You saw Ben identify these footprints as those of Laban Biggerman's slave."

The other men nodded, but Johnny kept his eyes open. When Cal was solemn, that was the time to watch out.

"Well, Ben," Cal drawled as he held out his wrists, "you may as well handcuff me now." Then he stepped into the footprints and posed like he was running. Anyone could see that Cal had made the footprints himself to trick Mitchell and Shoup.

Ben Mitchell's eyes bulged. "Here, now, what do you mean by this rigmarole?" His denial was feeble.

How Ripley men appreciated a good joke! Jolly Bob in particular doubled over with laughter as Johnny and Cal rejoined the crowd by the front door.

"So your slave is here at Rankin's, Biggerman?" Jolly Bob taunted. "I'd like to see you try to take Cal Rankin back with you. Oh, my!" He wiped tears from his eyes.

Biggerman raked Jolly Bob with a look of pure venom. The abolitionists far outnumbered the slave hunters by then. Their ridicule continued, some of the words more mean-spirited than Johnny was used to hearing. Yet every minute that Biggerman remained here gave the refugee that much more of a head start.

At last Biggerman's temper boiled over. Johnny shivered to recall his words. "The slaves know what you do, and so do we." He spat tobacco juice. "You—must—be—stopped. I don't care what I have to do. I will destroy you." His calmness chilled Johnny. "And if I can't find you, why, then"—he waved a hand down the hill—"I will burn Ripley to the ground, and I will shed no tears over that festering sore of an abolition hole." He spat again. "But above all else, if I should only see that fine preacher, Mr. John Rankin, in an early grave, I shall be well content."

That's when Johnny heard a click and a quiet "Out of my way, boys." Mother stepped forward, brandishing a rifle. Biggerman ducked, and the crowd quieted. "You lurk around our house and spy on us. We never lock our door, and many's the time you've searched the house in our absence." Biggerman grunted, but she nodded. "You know that's the truth, yet you've found no slaves.

Keep away from here or feel the force of powder and lead. If no one else will shoot, I shall do it myself."

Laban Biggerman glared, but Mother did not budge. The slave hunters beat a hasty retreat, but from that moment on, life on the hill changed.

Johnny snapped out of his reverie. Oh, yes, life had changed. Father demanded caution and vigilance, and the reappearance of this slave woman meant a fine mess to sort out. If anyone outside the family saw her, she could be legally forced back to Kentucky for a reward, even now. Johnny stepped over the potato plants and trotted to warn Father and Mother of the danger.

Still he puzzled it out—when *had* this slave come through? She'd had a baby with her then. Tom, the newest Rankin baby, had been born two years ago, but somehow it seemed that the river had iced over before that.

Ice—that was the key. He'd had to wait for all the ice to melt before he could travel to Cincinnati and Lane Seminary. He grinned. He had the time pegged now: 1838, the year Father had sent him to Lane for three months to keep him from telling anyone about . . .

Johnny's insides turned to water. Mrs. Stowe, Lyman Beecher's writer daughter—he'd told her about this very slave. To his mind, the slave woman was long gone, and it wouldn't matter if someone outside the family knew about her wondrous escape over the ice. He had never dreamed she'd come back.

He tried to slink back to the potato patch, but it was too late—Father had recognized the visitor. He stared at the pair with wide eyes before hustling everyone into the house. Mother fetched a dipper of water and waited until the visitors satisfied their thirst. She led the woman to the davenport in the front room and bade her sit down. "Well, Auntie, what has brought you back here?"

The slave clasped her hands. "I've come for my big girl and

her babies. They're right over there." She waved a hand toward Kentucky.

"Risk your freedom? You don't know what you're saying." Father's Sunday voice reached every corner of the house. In a matter of seconds, most of Johnny's brothers and sisters had edged into the front room to see the cause of such a ruckus.

"Yes, I do, oh, Mr. Rankin, I do know! I gots it all planned out in my mind." The slave gestured at the man in the strange outfit, and Johnny started—he'd forgotten about him. "He's a good hand to work. He can go over for a while, then bring my girl here." She slapped a fat leather pouch on the table. "I done saved all my money until there was enough to pay him, once he bring my babies back to me." Her dark eyes glowed with joy.

Father swung to scrutinize the strangely dressed man. "Preposterous! Those people know everyone for miles. You'd stick out like a sore thumb!"

The man had removed his hat, and Johnny saw that his eyes were steel blue. He made no effort to reply, however, and Johnny wondered if he understood English. He stole another glance at the trousers, buttoned to the pants just so. Father was right. Those clothes would be a dead giveaway.

Father's next remark wiped the smile from Johnny's face. "Furthermore, we do not carry the war into Kentucky." He crossed his arms.

The slave's face puckered. "Beg yo' pardon?"

Mother patted her arm. "What's your name, my dear?" she asked, and Johnny realized with a shock that none of them knew.

"My name is Eliza." She held her head high and proud.

"Well, Eliza, Mr. Rankin means it is too dangerous for you to go over to Kentucky." Johnny noticed Mother did not say it with much conviction.

Eliza looked at Reverend Rankin in disbelief. "No, sir." She shook her head. "Don't you tell me that. Every day I wonder how long 'til I hold my gal here again." She gestured at her heart. "Every day I pray for the good Lord to show me how. Praise be, one night He told me, 'Go!' and He done told me how. I got up the next morning, told Pastor Wilks my plans. Said he would watch George and Mose, so I kissed them and hired this man. 'Call me Gil,' he said. We walked so many weary miles from Canada, straight to this red brick house on the hill that I will never in this world forget. I been waiting to come back since Mose started talkin', and he almost four years old now." Eliza's lips trembled. "An' now you tell me I can't go?" She put her head down and bawled.

Mother knelt beside Eliza. Mother, whom Johnny had never seen shed a tear, was crying now. She draped her arm around Eliza's shoulders as her dream died before their eyes. "My girl, my girl! Oh, Lord," Eliza moaned and covered her eyes. "My Lord! It is too much to bear!"

Johnny sniffled. Surely Father would give in.

But Father didn't. "Eliza, you go over there and you're as good as sold down the river, and this man's certain to swing by the neck." Father crossed his arms. "Let me make it plain. He'll be dead, and you will wish you were."

Eliza looked up and held Father's gaze for a moment before she bowed her head again.

Then Mother spoke. "Are you absolutely certain, John?" Slowly Eliza's head came up, and her eyes blazed with new hope.

"Have you all forgotten what happened to John Mahan?"

Johnny *had* forgotten, but Mahan's name brought the memory back. Lowry had delivered a slave to the Reverend Mahan, who'd made the poor choice of keeping the slave for several days instead of immediately sending him north. Laban Biggerman had forcibly removed Mahan from his home. Mahan had then languished in the Washington, Kentucky jail for sixteen months, held on the trumped-up testimony of a deaf man who had indicated that Mahan had come to Kentucky to steal the slave.

"Dunlop finally paid his bail, John. Mahan is free."

"Yes, William Dunlop paid $1,600 rather than see John Mahan go to the state penitentiary. Dunlop is a fine anti-slavery man, but he is also a businessman. Mahan had to give up his property and everything he owned to Dunlop." Father paused for emphasis. "All Biggerman had to do was accuse Mahan of stealing one slave from Kentucky. We know for a fact that Mahan never set foot there, yet he's lost every penny, and his health is ruined, to boot. He's not long for this world. And now you want to help this woman steal her family away from Kentucky, Jean?" He shook his head. "I won't risk it. We could lose everything."

"That's just it, John." Mother held his gaze.

A smile played about Father's lips. "So you agree?"

Mother waved a hand, and Johnny turned. His brothers and sisters stood behind him. "We're talking about her *family*." She dabbed her eyes with the corner of her apron. "Look at Eliza. She's a Christian woman. See how she's dressed!"

One by one, the rest of the Rankins took in Eliza's tattered homespun jacket and trousers and ducked their heads. Johnny's cheeks flamed. Which was more outlandish, the Canadian man's clothing or a Christian grandmother dressed as a man? But Mother wasn't finished.

"You all heard her. She's left her husband and her son in the care of a friend. She's saved all her money for years to pay this man"—she gestured at the silent Gil—"for the privilege of having her daughter and grandchildren at her side." She reached her arm about Johnny's waist and drew him to her side. "I enjoy the same privilege as easy as this. She already *has* lost everything. She's—she's walked hundreds of miles to rescue her family. We cannot deny her that right. God will not deny her." Johnny felt Mother's hand tremble at his waist.

Gil clapped three times and gave a slight bow. "Magnificent, Madame." His steely eyes flashed. "You are a tigress."

For an instant, Mother was flustered, but she inclined her head with grace. "Thank you, sir. There, John, he speaks perfect English. With a change of clothes . . ."

Gil straightened. "As for my clothes, of course I would not wear the uniform of a French-Canadian sailor."

"See that you don't," Father retorted. "Those clothes would betray you on sight."

Eliza sat with her elbows on her knees, her face buried in her hands. Johnny wondered if she sensed that Father had given in a particle. It came to him with a fresh shock that he had betrayed this grandmother—to a writer. His insides squirmed again. He hoped Mrs. Stowe would honor her promise to keep the story a secret.

Then Eliza raised her head. "Thank you, Jesus," she whispered.

Johnny saw Sam stare hard. "I know you," he burst out. "You brought a man across one night, to get him away from Biggerman." Sam folded his arms across his chest and nodded.

Eliza's face lit up. "Yes, sir! That was my husband, George."

Father groaned. "So you helped your husband escape, you stole your baby away when you escaped, and now you want to liberate your daughter, who is with Mr. James—and Biggerman?"

"Oh, no, Beulah, she done got sold away from Mr. James after I helped George run off. Now she b'long to Mr. Adkins, over Germantown way. Leastaways, last I heard."

"That's small comfort. Biggerman won't have forgotten." Father's jaw twitched. "How many children does Beulah have?"

"Five." Johnny saw Mother flinch. Eliza hurried to add, "This gentleman here, Gil, he gonna scout out where she is and bring her and all five o' her children over here, though. Me and the good Lord has got it all planned out."

"Five! See here, far too many people know about you already, Eliza. Sam recognized you. If one of those children makes a peep and calls attention to us, it's over." Father shook his head.

"You leave the children to me," she reassured Father. "Way I figure, only worry we have, 'sides Biggerman hisself, is that man that let me and Mose go, down yonder by the river."

Johnny saw the memory of that night register. "Zeke Means," Father said weakly. "Zeke Means saw you, too. We have to hide you away this very night. Who else knows about you?"

"No one."

"Let's keep it that way." He scanned the room. "No one else," he said, and his gaze lingered on Johnny the longest, "is to know about Eliza."

Only Johnny knew that Father's warning was three years too late.

Chapter 10

ELIZA

"MADAME, YOU ARE A superb cook." Gil kissed his fingertips in appreciation. Eliza wondered if she would ever get used to his ways.

Mrs. Rankin thanked Gil and set her girls to cleaning the table. *Lawsy mercy, the Lord has blessed this family with a lot of children!* But the one Eliza noticed most was the scrawny one named Johnny. She looked at him. He looked away right quick, but his cheeks were burning red. Looked like he didn't feel good at all. Eliza patted the kerchief full of herbs she'd worn under her hat. That boy needed doctoring, and she made up her mind to speak to Mrs. Rankin about it later.

As soon as Mr. Rankin spoke, though, Eliza knew there would be no cozy chat with the preacher's wife after dinner. "Eliza, you will have to go to Arch Hopkins's place right away. No one ever bothers Arch."

Several of the children chuckled, and Eliza felt uneasy. Mrs. Rankin said, "Pay no mind to them. Arch wouldn't harm a fly. You couldn't have a better situation, either, right handy when your daughter gets over here."

Eliza breathed deep. Soon she would see Beulah; that was all that mattered.

Mr. Rankin gave Gil a measuring look. "Cal, run upstairs and see what clothes you can spare for this man." He asked Gil, "How long do you suppose it will take to get the lay of the land in Kentucky?"

"I have studied on this." Gil rubbed his chin. "I need to gain the confidence of the people, so I will get a job, perhaps as a woodchopper or some such. The steamboats always need wood." He indicated Eliza. "This one has told me the names of all the farmers and where they live, their habits, everything I need to know as we walked here." He looked at Mr. Rankin. "So I already have the 'lay of the land,' as you say."

Gil's answer seemed to mollify Mr. Rankin, but he had one more question. "How will you get over to Kentucky? We will not take you."

"Monsieur, I am a sailor in the French-Canadian navy. Only provide me with the use of a skiff, and I shall manage quite well."

Eliza saw mottled spots of red form high on Mr. Rankin's cheekbones. He looked like a cornered hound. "Look around you. Our very lives depend on your discretion, sir. Take every precaution so that you are not found out."

"I will certainly do so." Gil bowed ever so slightly.

Eliza puffed out her cheeks and exhaled.

"Cal, give him your clothes and help him get ready. He can use Mr. Collins's skiff—someone will bring it back when they want to come over here, just like always." Mr. Rankin was in command again. "Soon as you leave the Ripley shore, you are on your own. You are clever; you will find a way to get word to us, should you need to. Eliza," he said, "will go to Arch Hopkins's house right away. How much time do you think you will need, Gil?"

"Three months only."

"Three months. Then we shall expect you back here sometime after that to tell us your plan. Let us say by the first of October." Mr. Rankin sighed, as if that day seemed far away. "All right, boys, who will take Eliza down to Arch's place?"

Eliza peered at the brood of young men, close-grouped and sweaty in the airless room. *Now, what happened to that skinny little black-headed boy, Johnny?* She glimpsed the back of him just before he slipped out the front door.

"Johnny?" Mr. Rankin said. "Going out to get Old Sorrel ready? That's fine; you may take Eliza as soon as we get her clothes befitting a Christian woman. You saw her that first night after she crossed on the ice, so it's fitting that her welfare should be your responsibility." Mr. Rankin beamed like he was doing the boy a favor. "You've gotten so you can hold your tongue. I know we can trust you to keep her secret, and you've waited a long time to be captain. Here is your chance at last."

God has a pleasant way of workin' things out, Eliza mused. Johnny was the very one she wanted. Yessir, there were smiles all around at this turn of events, except from Johnny—he looked a little green around the gills. Likely something he ate had disagreed with him, but she could tell him what herbs would fix him up while they were on the way to the Hopkins place.

After words of warning from Mr. Rankin and well wishes from the rest of the family, Gil headed south toward the river, and Eliza and Johnny traveled north. Old Sorrel trailed Johnny's horse, and Eliza settled down for three miles of hard riding. Soon Johnny nudged his horse to take a cutoff that looked like a rabbit track through thick brush, and Old Sorrel stepped lightly to follow.

It looked like the reason no one ever bothered Arch Hopkins was that few would be able to reach his place. The woods pressed in around the path. Eliza sweltered beneath the herb-laden kerchief. She'd be a sight if the herbs steeped and tea ran down into her eyes. Johnny gallantly broke through the worst of the cobwebs and vines, but Eliza brushed plenty of sticky strands from her face. She could not shake the feeling that a scratchy-legged black spider might crawl down her neck.

"Where in tarnation does this trail let out?" she asked at last.

Johnny laughed, and Eliza saw his spine unstiffen a mite. He waved his arm. "Almost anywhere."

"You sure we goin' the right way?"

"Yes, ma'am. And even if I didn't know the way, Old Sorrel does. Mr. Hopkins sold him to us."

A scuffle erupted in the underbrush. Johnny's horse shied and Old Sorrel jerked his head upright to avoid a collision. He stretched his neck and whinnied. From the corner of her eye, Eliza saw a flash of white; a cottontail rabbit scooted under the belly of Johnny's horse and into the thicket. The leaves whipped into place behind it, and once more a deep woods hush settled.

Eliza lifted the reins, but before Old Sorrel raised a hoof, she gasped. A fox the color of sunburn trickled between the two horses, right under Old Sorrel's nose. Old Sorrel stretched his neck and snapped. Eliza saw a few black guard hairs from the fox's brush catch in the horse's teeth, but the fox rippled after the rabbit like water over mossy stones.

"Are you all right, Auntie?" the boy asked. He turned around in the saddle and watched her with anxious, gray eyes.

"Yes, sir, Mr. John. I done saw a fox chase after a rabbit, that's all." She grinned to reassure him, and he urged his horse forward. "You better watch out or he'll come around some night and steal y'all's chickens, you hear?"

Johnny chuckled, but Eliza clutched Old Sorrel's reins with clammy hands. She recalled another rabbit, the one the owl had snatched up a few nights before she and Mose crossed the ice. The woods were full of creatures that would gobble up a rabbit easier than she could turn over her hand. This close to Kentucky, the old anxiety returned—she was just a river away from her old life of slavery. Eliza closed her eyes. *Lord, don't let me get caught like that little old rabbit. Watch over me.*

At last they rode downhill through the shoulder-to-shoulder

ranks of trees on the hills that ringed the Hopkins farm. Gray-green leaves hung limp as the horses shambled into the hollow.

"Here we are. Father says not even a breeze can find the Hopkins place." Johnny pulled up his horse. Eliza saw a two-story farmhouse with a wide porch and two windows on either side of the front door. An old barn built of massive plastered logs towered to one side.

"I ain't a-going to bite you."

The light in the sun-dazzled hollow blinded Eliza. She squinted to see a little old man with hair as white as the rabbit's tail. His hands were clasped across his round belly as he sat on the porch in a chair tipped to lean against the brick wall. The front chair legs crashed to the boards and he grimaced. He eased to his feet, planted a hand against a post, and cocked a hip that must have pained him some. He frowned at Eliza.

"That's Mr. Hopkins," Johnny muttered. "His broken hip makes him crotchety."

The man cupped his hands around his mouth. "Not deaf yet, Johnny Rankin. Who be your friend?"

Johnny curved his neck so that his hat made a barrier between his face and Mr. Hopkins's line of sight. "He can talk the hind leg off a donkey," he whispered. His gray eyes gleamed; whatever had been troubling the boy's insides must have passed off.

Eliza grinned—the boy sure had spunk. She fanned herself with her hat as Johnny introduced her. "This is Eliza, sir. Father has some instructions for you." He fumbled in his pocket.

"You tell me what he wants, boy," Mr. Hopkins interrupted. A chuckle shook his belly. "'Go ask Johnny.' That's what they say in Ripley, ain't it?"

Eliza saw Johnny flinch like a whip had struck him. He thrust the note at Mr. Hopkins without another word. Something was bothering that boy again, bothering him so bad it made her heart hurt. He reminded her of Shad somehow. She wanted to take him under her wing and protect him from Mr. Hopkins's sharp tongue.

The old man held the paper at arm's length. His lips moved until he finished reading. The paper crackled as he creased it and put it in his pocket. He looked Eliza up and down. "Can you cook?"

She rested a fist on her thigh. "Reckon I can." It was hard to talk with her teeth gritted together.

Mr. Hopkins reared his head back in surprise. He scrutinized her some more. "You get along good with people, or would you rather sass 'em?"

"I gets along with people just fine when they behaves like good Christians." She slitted her eyes at him.

Mr. Hopkins drew himself up and pursed his lips to speak, but gentle words interrupted him.

"Now, would our pastor get up on his high horse like that, Archibald?"

The old man jerked his head toward the open door, and all the fight ebbed from his stance. He looked like his hip was painin' him again.

A large, handsome woman with a single gray braid emerged from the house with stately grace. She took hold of Old Sorrel's bridle. "Let me help you down."

Eliza unhooked her knee from the pommel and slid off Old Sorrel's back. She staggered across the porch and put a hand on the brick wall. Her legs would be permanently bowed if she kept on riding horses.

The lady handed the reins over to Johnny. "Howdy do, Johnny. How's your folks?"

"They're well, Mrs. Hopkins." The boy smiled and leaned to give her a hug. "This is Eliza. She's come to help you and Miss Harriet out for the next three months."

"I'm glad to hear it! We can use some help with baking while we start the canning. Of course, we'll pay you." She nodded at her chastened husband. "Archibald slipped on this icy porch two winters ago, and it took forever for the bone to knit," she confided to Eliza. "He's all bluster when his hip hurts, but he don't mean no harm."

Mr. Hopkins mustered a scowl. "Tut, tut, Margie . . ."

Mrs. Hopkins smiled at her husband, and his sputtering subsided. "Bye, bye, Johnny. Come back soon." A deep glow of contentment shone from Mrs. Hopkins's eyes. She linked arms with Eliza. "Now come with me, honey."

"I'll be back as quick as we get word," Johnny said.

Mr. Hopkins grunted. "Long's you're coming back, you can bring me the newspaper when your folks get done with it." He glanced at his wife and added, "Please."

Johnny grinned at that. "I'll do that. See you soon, Auntie," he called. He chirruped, and Old Sorrel stomped and twitched his tawny hide to dislodge a horsefly. He fell in behind Johnny's horse and the trio left the hollow.

꘎

July crawled into August, and Eliza often thought that the minute she watched Johnny ride away was the last idle one she spent with Mrs. Hopkins. The woman never stopped working; her spinster daughter was just as tireless.

Harriet Hopkins was big and rawboned like her mother. Privately Eliza thought Harriet would never make a glorious old woman like Mrs. Hopkins. For one thing, she was as awkward as a colt. She had a spray of freckles across her bony nose and a horsey laugh that always startled the daylights out of Eliza. No two ways about it, Harriet was plain.

Harriet looked so much like a horse that it seemed fitting she loved horses as much as her father did. Old Archie, as Eliza called him in her mind, set great store by this daughter who had stayed with him and Margie in their old age. Old Archie and Harriet rode everywhere together, the old man on his beloved saddle mare, Bonny, and the faithful daughter mounted on some "suitable riding creature." Old Archie was a fearless rider and Harriet was his match. Both rode sidesaddle, Old Archie to spare his ill-mended hip, and Harriet because her father said, "No proper lady rides astraddle."

August passed slowly in Hopkins Hollow—except on Saturdays; there weren't enough hours in a Saturday. Old Archie had a strict rule to honor the Sabbath, so all the Sunday meals had to be prepared the day before. That meant all-day cooking because every Hopkins child came home for supper after church.

Eliza went to church with the family, too, because Old Archie decreed that no one in his house was going to miss church, danger or no. Eliza attended the services with her face far back in her bonnet, bundled in a long-sleeved dress and gloves. She was hotter than fire, but she enjoyed the preaching. Mrs. Hopkins proved wise to govern her husband by mentioning the minister, as he was the only person on earth to whom Old Archie deferred. To Eliza's surprise, he was Pastor Gilliland of Red Oak, the selfsame man she'd stayed with after she'd left the Rankins the first time.

It tickled her something fierce that a humble man like Pastor Gilliland had a hold over Old Archie, who reminded her of a banty rooster. Once, a Hopkins daughter-in-law had referred to her husband as Mr. Hopkins. Old Archie had cut in to say, "Tut, tut, there is only one Mr. Hopkins in this family. *I'm* Mr. Hopkins." Yet Eliza knew that Old Archie had not even let his children marry without meek Pastor Gilliland's say-so.

It seemed funny to call them children; the sons were imposing figures, like their mother. They brought their wives and families to church every Sunday and gathered at Old Archie's house after the services for a huge meal. Eliza spent Saturdays baking for the big feast, and here it was, Saturday again. She worked in the kitchen with a great clattering of pans.

One thing Old Archie had to admit: the sweet potato rolls Eliza baked for Sunday breakfast beat the featherbed rolls his dear departed mother used to make. Eliza could see him now, drizzling hot butter over them and closing his eyes for a big bite before church.

She poked the boiled potatoes; yes, they were fork tender. Billows of steam moistened her face as she drained the pot. With the tines of a fork, she mashed the potatoes fine and mealy. *Lawsy mercy, sometimes seems like I done spent my whole life in one steamy kitchen or another, cooking for a big family.*

Tears welled up without warning. The last of August already, with no word from the Rankins about Gil. It was so hard to wait three months, harder even than the past three years. She sniffed and rubbed her eyes with the back of a hand. When would she see Beulah and her children again?

Good thing she was so busy, after all. She pushed back her worries and sifted flour over the potatoes. The cinnamon and nutmeg made her sneeze as she measured in a pinch. The humid air had rendered the sugar into a hard block, and she had to chip off enough for sweetening. She added in a spoonful of yeast and kneaded to her heart's content—wonderful to muscle the dough into a smooth mass. She whisked a checkered cloth over the bowl and set the dough to rise. This afternoon, she would punch it down and work in a piece of butter. Last of all, she'd shape the dough into small rolls before she baked them.

She smacked her lips. Oh, how Shad always teased her for a sweet potato roll, hot from the pan! *Shad . . .* and then she dissolved in tears.

Those bright-eyed children, where are they, Lord? Has something gone wrong? She groped blindly for a chair and felt a hand on her shoulder. She choked back a sob; steadfast Harriet was at her side. Eliza hadn't known a body could look so kind. Harriet wasn't the least bit awkward, either, as she hugged Eliza. Somehow, this homely woman *understood*. After all, she had chosen to stay with her parents in their old age rather than to make a home of her own. Love bubbled up to soothe Eliza's heart. After a while, she returned to her baking.

The warm glow carried her through until church the next morning. Sundays hurt; the Hopkins children, grandchildren, and great-grandchildren lined the pews at Red Oak Church, one big, happy family. Eliza eased forward a bit to catch a glimpse of Mrs. Hopkins, who held two babies on her lap. *Happy woman!*

Before she knew it, Eliza felt weepy again. She bit her lip and longed to see a familiar face, someone who loved *her*.

Old Archie always drove like Jehu to beat the rest of the family home from church. When the last carriage rumbled up to the Hopkins homestead, the family gathered under the trees to wait patiently for Harriet and Old Archie to come up from the barn. Finally, Eliza saw a white head and a chestnut mane as Old Archie limped beside his daughter. She whispered something in his ear. Then everyone bowed their heads and Old Archie asked the blessing.

Eliza's stomach growled as the prayer stretched; must the man pray for everyone in Brown County and beyond? 'Sides, she knew what came next in his windy prayers: he always thanked God for keeping his family close. Eliza gritted her teeth, but his next words took her breath away.

"Dear Lord, we ask Your blessing on everyone here, most especially on Eliza, whose family has been torn asunder. We ask You, whose eye is on the sparrow, to watch over her family and keep them safe. Bring them back together soon and very soon, Lord, if it be Your will. Comfort Eliza's heart while she waits. In Jesus' name we pray, Amen."

When she opened her eyes, it was like a gentle rain had blessed her parched soul. Old Archie was already heaping plates with cold fried chicken, but Harriet held Eliza's gaze as two big tears rolled down her cheeks. Eliza was not alone, after all. She would always be a part of God's family, even if she never saw Beulah and her children again.

Monday morning, Eliza sat on the porch with a bowl on her lap and a mess of string beans piled over an old newspaper on the chair next to her. She heard a plaintive whinny and jumped out of her chair. Beans scattered over the porch. Just before Eliza ducked in the front door, a scrawny black cat streaked across her path, right into the house. What better sign did she need that trouble was coming?

Old Archie heard the horse, too, and blustered out on the porch. Eliza hid behind Mrs. Hopkins's freshly laundered curtains and scanned the wreath of hills.

She spotted the horse before she could make out the rider; the animal was a bright bay with shiny, black legs. The fine head drooped; why, that horse was plumb miserable. Well, horseflies were bad enough to drive a beast to distraction. Thank the good Lord He had given horses manes and tails.

What in this world? Eliza squinted. That horse *had* no mane. Close-cropped black bristles ridged its neck. The poor animal had no silky topknot to toss over its eyes, just a black sprout shorter than a scrub brush. When the bay angled toward the house, hot tears spilled over Eliza's cheeks. Where the horse should have switched a long, black tail, she saw a stub like a bony finger that didn't even reach the horse's hocks. But the worst injustice of all was that one ear had been lopped clean off.

Eliza clenched her fists, ready to do battle with whoever would hurt a defenseless animal like that. Just then the rider raised his head and waved a bundle of newspapers. At long last, Johnny Rankin had come to call.

Chapter 11

Johnny

Johnny patted the bay's damp neck as he rode up to the house. "You're all right, old fellow." He shooed flies off Elijah's flanks with a leafy hickory twig.

The door creaked, and Eliza joined Mr. Hopkins on the porch. Her eyes were red and she sniffled. She nodded and knelt to pick up the scattered string beans, which lay in a splash of green at their feet. Johnny watched her shoot a sidelong glance at the horse, like it spooked her some.

"Johnny Rankin, what in tarnation happened to your father's horse this time?" Mr. Hopkins glared at him.

"Mornin', Mr. Hopkins." Johnny dismounted and delivered the bundle of newspapers. "Father's been preaching abolition over to Manchester. Someone shaved Elijah's mane and tail again last night during the service. He came home to trade horses, but he's going back to Manchester."

Mr. Hopkins flicked at flies clustered on the horse's reddish-brown neck. He stuck out his lower lip and brooded.

"Who'd do that to a helpless critter?" Eliza's eyes fairly sparked.

"Slave hunters, Father says." It was on the tip of his tongue to add that Biggerman was most likely behind the attack, but instead he turned to Mr. Hopkins. "Do any of your horses need their tails thinned? Father figures we can loop a makeshift tail over the base, just to get Elijah through fly season."

"Harriet!" Mr. Hopkins bawled so suddenly that Elijah nearly jumped out from under Johnny. When his daughter appeared, he said, "Run out to the barn and thin some tails to braid a switch for him." He jerked a thumb at Elijah, who snorted and showed the whites of his eyes. Harriet took one look at the horse and jumped off the high porch to lead him to shelter.

"Mr. Rankin needs to call that poor horse Elisha 'stead of Elijah." It was Eliza who spoke. Amusement flickered through Johnny, but Mr. Hopkins scowled at the woman.

"What you flapping your gums about, 'Liza?"

Eliza sat down with the stoneware bowl on her lap and the beans near at hand. Johnny watched her deliberately peel the strings from the tips of a bean and snap it into sections faster than even Mother could. She plinked them into the bowl and her chin came up. "Heard Pastor Gilliland say yesterday that the prophet Elisha was a baldhead." She bent over the bowl so far that only her red kerchief was visible.

"You get back to work," Mr. Hopkins growled.

"Mr. Hopkins, sir, I ain't stopped working. I'm just saying what Pastor Gilliland said."

"See to it that I get string beans for my supper, you hear?"

"Yes, sir, I hear."

Johnny rubbed his lip to hold back a chuckle and flopped into a green ladder-back chair beside Eliza. Mr. Hopkins's face was a study as he thrust the newspapers under his arm and stumped into the house.

A string bean flew from Eliza's hand. Johnny smiled as a half-wild tabby kitten nipped onto the porch to inspect it with round eyes. He picked up the bean and offered it to the kitten, which sniffed it with whiskers swept back. The kitten growled low in its throat, sank a baby fang into the tough, green shell, and scampered away with the treasure.

Eliza sat up and rubbed her red eyes.

"Mr. Hopkins treating you right, Auntie?"

She tucked a crinkly strand of gray hair under her kerchief and gave a half-hearted nod. Her mouth puckered. "Sometimes I feel like I ain't never gonna see my girl and my grandbabies again."

"It won't be much longer," he reassured. "I saw Gil in town today."

"You saw him?" Eliza gripped his arm.

I should have told her right away. "He's lost some weight. And he looks just like all the other men in Ripley now—no more trousers buttoned to his jacket."

She sat up straight; she reminded Johnny of a queen on her throne. "What did he say?"

"He's found your daughter." She gave a sharp cry, and he rushed on, "All the children are well, he says." At least he hoped that was what Gil's curt nod had meant.

Eliza thrust the bowl of string beans at him and hid her face in her apron for a moment. "Oh, thank You, Lord! Thank You!"

Johnny swallowed hard and cast about for any other tidbits he had gleaned from the grapevine telegraph. "He told me he works for a farmer who is clearing bottomland for tobacco. He was in town to sell a load of wood to the steamboats."

Eliza puffed out her cheeks. She dabbed eyes that were as shiny as black coffee and said, "Oh, I wish I could see George and Mose right now, to tell them." Gently she held Johnny's face between her hands. He caught a pleasant whiff of cinnamon and spice. "You brought me good news, honey. I been working for this day for three years. Soon my whole family gonna be together again, and then we gonna have us a jubilee!"

She retrieved the bowl of beans. Her tremulous smile wrenched Johnny's heart and shamed him at the same time. Soon as he woke up in the morning, his family was there, and many were the times he had grumbled over their number. Ibby had moved away with her husband, but they were not far—the next farm over. Even Lowry and Mandy roomed with the Rankins while Lowry traveled to fill other pulpits until he got his own church. Eliza had no one close at hand.

"I just hope in my heart don't nobody figure out Beulah's gone before we get back here," Eliza continued. She shook her head. "I don't want that Biggerman to come nosin' around."

"Don't you worry. Gil will never let on." Johnny thought about the Frenchman's curt nod and brightened. "He can keep a secret ever so well, same as Mr. Hopkins. No one will find out about you."

Oh, yes, somebody will, because you already blabbed her story. The thought welled up unbidden, so close on the heels of his promise that it left him breathless. Eliza trusted him with her whole heart, and he did not deserve it.

"I have to go," he muttered as he quickly got to his feet. "Tell Mr. Hopkins I walked home."

"How 'bout your horse?"

He chopped the air with a dismissive gesture. "Somebody will get him."

Eliza laid a hand on his shoulder. "God bless you, Johnny. Come back and see me soon. You's almost like family."

As soon as he was under cover of the trees, Johnny picked up a stick and hacked at leaves. Blind rage fueled his steps. Yes, he'd told Mrs. Stowe about Eliza. So what? That was three whole years ago. He had certainly kept his mouth shut since. Even though he was under strict orders to keep the family's work a secret, the slaveholders knew about it anyway. Hadn't the finger of blame pointed indirectly at Father last week when every one of Simon Nichols's slaves had run off?

Earlier in the week, some wag had asked one of Nichols's slaves, "Why don't you stay here, now that you are in Ohio?" He'd answered, "No, sir, I will never go away from Master

Nichols!" But by the time the moon had set the next morning, Simon Nichols no longer had a slave to his name—they had all run off.

The problem had started when Nichols trusted his slaves to do business in Ripley without supervision. They put the time to good use. Soon word circulated through the grapevine telegraph that Nichols's slaves frequently assisted other slaves over the river and sent them to Father's house. When the other slaveholders found out, they formed a committee and brought the matter before Nichols.

Nichols had been in a tight spot—he truly loved his slaves, but what could he do? They had been stealing valuable property, so he decided to sell them.

The grapevine telegraph worked both ways, however. By the time Nichols made arrangements with Biggerman, his slaves had run off to freedom themselves.

Nichols had tracked his property with surprising speed as far as Cleveland. There he'd watched as his slaves scrambled aboard a schooner that set sail across Lake Erie for Canada and freedom. Johnny wished he could have seen that sight, yet the news had sobered the Rankins.

Nichols had returned home fighting mad, and since he no longer had the guilty parties under ownership, his ire had turned to someone who was always handy—the Rankin family.

Johnny hurled the stick. All his family had ever done was help men and women to freedom. *There's nothing wrong with that.* In fact, doing it made him feel so good that he wanted to tell the whole world, especially about Eliza's escape over the ice. But instead, he'd told only Mrs. Stowe, and she'd promised never to reveal his family's secret.

Yet, far from being recognized for heroism, the Rankins were marked for revenge. Last night, someone had raided a nearby lumberyard and dragged huge beams to the church during the vesper service. Somehow they had propped them against the front doors. If Father had pulled the big doors open at the end of the service, as was his custom, the massive timbers would have crushed him like a deer in a deadfall, and the happy marauders would have been three thousand dollars richer. That was the bounty on Father's head—dead or alive, with "dead" definitely preferred.

Thank God that a friend had slipped out of a neighboring church a couple of minutes before the benediction. The friend had spotted the timbers, waited until the last organ note sounded, and then immediately popped his head in the side door and warned the congregation to avoid the front exit until the deadfall was cleared away.

Lowry had preached that night in Father's place. If not for that friend, Lowry would have been a dead man. At about the same time last night, Elijah's mane and tail had been shorn while Father preached in Manchester.

What thanks did Johnny's family have for their many sacrifices? In the weeks since Eliza had returned, hardly a night had passed without men prowling around the Rankin home. Surely it was only a matter of time before somebody slipped up and the slave hunters could prove that the family helped slaves escape. That's when real trouble was bound to come.

Maybe things would get better after they sent Eliza back home. How his family was going to keep Eliza's second escape a secret, with five clamoring children to smuggle away, was more than Johnny could bear to think about right now.

By the time he realized he'd missed the cutoff for home, Johnny could already hear the creak of wagon wheels and the chatter that meant town. The soothing noise quelled the insistent *"You betrayed her"* that haunted his thoughts.

"Hello, there!"

Johnny stopped in his tracks. He knew every voice in Ripley, and this one was a trifle brighter than usual. He pushed back his hat and squinted. Sure enough, his classmate Mary Ann Hay beckoned from her front porch.

"I haven't seen you since school let out," she gushed. "Come up and talk to me a while." She crooked her finger.

Johnny's jaw dropped. Mary Ann was the least talkative girl in school; matter of fact, she usually just stared at him. Right now, she twirled the end of her coppery braid and beamed like she'd taken leave of her senses.

"Come on, now!" A bashful giggle followed. "I have something to tell you."

Mary Ann flirted for all she was worth, in plain view of most everyone in Ripley. Johnny's fickle feet stumbled up the steps until he faced her, his back to the street.

Mary Ann leaned toward him—she was even prettier up close. His stomach felt like the time he had dropped a stone into the well—it took a long time for the *plunk*.

She batted amber eyes flecked with gold. "I want you to know"—her whisper tickled his ear and made him squirm—"that Laban Biggerman is behind you, and he's been asking questions about Nichols's runaways."

Johnny froze. He searched her eyes; she meant it, and what's more, she looked scared to death.

"What do you think of that?" She clasped his hands and giggled loud enough for Biggerman to hear.

"Fine." Johnny forced himself to breathe as he mouthed, "Where?"

She shifted her eyes to a point not far beyond his shoulder. He could hear Biggerman now.

"Tell me the truth," the slave trader wheedled. "Suppose a body wanted to smoke out a fugitive. Y'all got a hidey hole somewheres in Ripley for runaways like Simon Nichols's boys, right?"

A second man snickered. "Nawww, I don't think so. But I'll

tell you what—if you want to know anything that's going on in Ripley . . ."

Johnny closed his eyes. *No.*

"Well, what?" Biggerman prodded, his rusty voice eager.

"Go ask Johnny."

Mary Ann squeezed his hands so hard that he opened his eyes and read secrets in hers. Her palms warmed his icy fingers.

"Johnny who?"

The second man hawked and spat. "Johnny Rankin, fool!" The tavern door squeaked and slammed.

Then Johnny heard nothing but the measured tread of Biggerman's feet. He knew, even without looking, that the slave trader was approaching. He cast about in his memory—would Biggerman recognize him?

The porch step creaked. Mary Ann pleaded with Johnny without saying a word. Then she leaned toward him until her bonnet hid his face. She tilted her head to one side, closed her eyes, and pressed her lips to his.

A low whistle split the air. "Sorry to intrude, little darlin'." There was a pause. "Sure wish I could get me some of that," the slave trader jeered. The step creaked again.

Mary Ann's hands trembled. She opened one eye. Her lips clung to Johnny's for the barest instant. "He's gone." She turned to peer between the hearts and trumpets of the morning glory vine that twined around the porch post. Slowly she released his numb fingers. "You're safe," she said. "Better hurry home."

His heart hammered as he edged backward. The heel of his boot dipped over nothing and he almost tumbled down the steps. "Th-thank you."

Mary Ann turned to fuss over her knitting basket, shoulders stiff. She stabbed the needles through a red ball of yarn and her skirts whirled as she faced him again. There were no secrets in her eyes now. "Don't you dare tell anyone I kissed you, Johnny Rankin."

"I won't," he whispered. "I promise."

Caution and vigilance. Johnny could almost hear Father's watchwords. He raced home on wobbly legs to tell him about Biggerman, but then he remembered—Father had gone back to Manchester. By the time he pushed open the front door, he was so worried for Father's safety that he had almost forgotten about Mary Ann.

Mother took one look at his face and demanded, "What's wrong, Johnny?"

"Biggerman's in town. He . . . I think . . . Father . . ."

And then, to Johnny's eternal relief, Father himself came into the room.

"I thought you'd gone back to Manchester already. I thought—" Johnny stammered.

"Easy, son." Father patted his back. "First things first. What about Biggerman?"

"I saw him. He thinks we know something about Simon Nichols's slaves."

"So we do." Father smiled. "Biggerman and his men have been hanging around town for a few days. Cal told me all about it; how he saw a group of shady characters at Ross's Hotel when he squired America Whisner home to Eagle Creek after church. I thought they would go home, but it makes no real difference that they didn't. I told Cal, and I'm telling you, that I forbid you or any of your brothers to molest those men unless you catch them in the act of doing us harm."

"But you didn't hear—"

"Now, Johnny. Watch and pray, that's the key." Father's tone was kind. "Thanks to some timely intervention, no real harm was done last night except to my horse Elijah, and we've found out that it's not permanent—he rides the same, though I regret the pain he's borne. If there is trouble, we are prepared. I have taken precautions." He stressed the last word. "I nailed the windows shut this afternoon, and now no one can easily get into our house. We are armed, but we will not shoot first. Eliza's safe at Arch's place. And what is more," Father added, "I believe I hear rain. You know we never have trouble when the weather is inclement."

Johnny swallowed. He had to admit, Father had thought of everything. The one thing he didn't know was that his son had not kept his mouth shut about Eliza. Maybe Biggerman didn't know about her, either. But what if he did?

The rain tapered to a sprinkle, then to steam. Supper was unbearably hot with the windows shut. For a long time after the meal, Johnny sat on the back steps and kept a silent vigil. Once in a while, he brushed a fingertip across lips that still tingled pleasantly. He watched the sunset color the sky like cream poured over a saucer of fresh strawberries—the color of Mary Ann's lips, come to think of it. He smiled.

Shafts of gold reflected off low, dark clouds and gilded the motionless leaves. The grass glistened with raindrops. Johnny pulled off his shoes and sat on the bottom step to drabble his feet in the coolness while he slapped at mosquitoes.

The twilight deepened until the silhouettes of trees stood out in sharp relief, black against violet. The mosquitoes hummed and feasted gladly on Johnny's arms and neck, but he knew a fate worse than mosquito bites, and that was roasting in his bed on a hot August night with the windows nailed shut.

Chuck.

He was on his feet before the sound died, fists clenched. He scanned the cornfield, the potato patch, the barn, the woods—nothing.

Whip-poor-will, whip-poor-will.

A wry grin cut the tension. At least no one had seen him jump. Again the whip-poor-will called to his mate, and she responded. They were so close that even the initial *chuck* of their song was clear, but their symphony was brief. They must have located each other.

He could put it off no longer—time to go in. A tickle at the tip of his nose stopped him, like he was about to run into something. He caught a glimpse of a compact body outlined against the lingering light. A whip-poor-will swooped and narrowly missed him, close enough to touch as it scooped Johnny's personal swarm of mosquitoes into its mouth. Now he saw the pair of birds swirl on noiseless wings, and then the wonder was over. The whip-poor-wills flew off together and sang no more. There was no need.

Johnny stretched. Whip-poor-wills were as good as a clock; he'd never heard them call between bedtime and two in the morning. He sighed and headed for the stuffy bedroom he shared with all his brothers but Lowry, who had moved to a downstairs bedroom with Mandy. David had taken a flatboat of timber down to New Orleans. Quick as David left, though, Cousin J.P. had come to fill up the empty spot.

The house was hotter than a stoked lime kiln. The very air sweltered and pressed the breath out of his lungs. Even the glow of the signal lantern added to the heat. Sweat stung Johnny's eyes and his damp nightshirt stuck to him as he climbed into bed. He threw off the smothery bedclothes, but Sam grunted in his sleep and flipped them back.

Johnny squinted at Cal and J.P., both fully dressed. When the clock struck midnight, the pair shucked off their coats and vests and draped them across a chair. Johnny heard the thump of boots and saw a flash of white as Cal wriggled his bare toes.

"You gonna stay awake?" J.P. asked.

Cal drawled, "You bet your life I am."

Johnny grinned. The last sight he saw before he fell asleep was Cal and J.P., their heads propped up on their fists, listening.

When the clock struck one, Johnny's head jerked. He strained his eyes; Cal stood by the window. A whip-poor-will called again.

"That ain't no whip-poor-will," J.P. whispered. "That's trouble. Let's go." He and Cal reached in their vest pockets, and the lantern light flashed on metal—guns. Cal stumbled over boots, but he didn't take time to put his on, and neither did J.P. Instead, the two boys pushed open the door and stole down the stairs, barefooted. Johnny heard the fourth step squeak, just like it always did after a rain. Then he heard nothing, and he knew his brother and cousin were out in the still August night.

Johnny crawled out of bed and blew out the lantern. He pressed his cheek to the window, a picture of caution and vigilance.

He didn't have to wait long. He heard Cal shout, "Halt!" A star of yellow light blossomed against the darkness, followed by a puff of smoke and a *crack*. Another shot echoed, and then a wail rose to a hoarse scream and stopped.

A thrill of horror twisted in Johnny's belly. In his mind's eye, he imagined Cal, so full of life only moments ago, stretched out on the ground as he stared at the clouds while his eyes glazed over. He could almost see his brother's hand cupped to his heart, see the blood that oozed between his fingers as his life pumped away to nothing.

Gunshots smote the air again. Johnny forced himself to watch as two figures fired at each other and scrambled for the fence. One of them hopped it and thumped to the ground with a scream before he slithered down the stony ravine.

Johnny dressed and clattered downstairs before his other brothers could pepper him with questions. The first person he saw was Mandy, clad in her nightgown, her hair frazzled up like spun flax and her arms wrapped so tight around Lowry's neck that he was red in the face.

"Let me go, Mandy." Lowry shrugged off her embrace, hooked

a thumb under one suspender and lifted it over his shoulder. His bootlaces trailed as he headed for the open door.

Johnny touched Mandy's arm. When she saw him, whatever fragile courage had sustained her dissolved. She collapsed into his arms and sobbed; he felt mighty like crying himself.

Then Mother burst from her bedroom and billowed down the stairs in a cloud of white nightclothes. She skimmed the landing, pushed past Lowry before he knew what was happening, slammed the door shut, and turned the key. "You're not leaving this house, Lowry. I won't allow it!" Her voice rose with each word.

Mandy's grateful sigh was a lovely sound like a prayer.

"Please, Mother, open the door!"

"Lowry, I shall not allow them to kill you, too." She glared up at Johnny. "Who's out there?"

"Cal and J.P."

She shook a finger at Lowry. "You see? A son and a nephew are enough for those brutes to steal from us. No one else shall leave this house!"

Boots thundered as more brothers thumped down the stairs.

Sam, ever gentle with Mother, tried quiet charm. "Please, Mother. I know you mean well, but we mustn't let them get away!"

"What if Cal and J.P. are only injured? We may save their lives!" Lowry went for the jugular.

It was a telling blow. Hope flared, but Johnny saw it die. Mother bit her lip and shook her head. "We can't take that chance."

Now the girls and the younger children crowded the steps. Julia bore a candle, and the light showed the girls' stricken faces. They scooped their terrified younger brothers and sisters into hugs partly meant to reassure themselves.

Floorboards creaked. At the head of the stairs, Johnny saw Father, fully dressed and in command. Immediately, Lowry and Sam switched tactics, but Johnny held his peace and watched.

"Oh, Father, Cal's been shot!"

"Mother does not understand—we must go out immediately!"

"Please tell her, Father!"

"She will listen to you!"

Father descended the stairs to stand beside Mother, his face drawn. He rumpled his hair and swallowed hard. "No. I heard seven shots fired before I got out of bed . . ." An eighth shot echoed, and they all shuddered at the answering scream.

"My Lord." Mother pressed the back of her hand to her mouth.

Father added shakily, "We can do the dead no good, so our next duty is to preserve the living."

The quiet that followed spooked them more than the awful scream. Mother remained dry-eyed as she shepherded the youngest children to her room, but Father's tears wet his cheeks. He rubbed his hands together as if he could not get warm.

Johnny eyed Lowry. He didn't know what his plan was, but he'd never seen Lowry left flat-footed at the start. His oldest brother was the one to watch, and this time, Johnny didn't intend to be left behind.

Sure enough, Lowry didn't hurry, and he didn't try to hide. He just walked to the front room like it was nobody's business but his own. Johnny retreated to the shadows and followed his lead. He watched his brother grip the sash and pull. The nails held; the window did not budge. Then Sam appeared beside Lowry, quiet as a whip-poor-will in flight. Together they threw their weight against the sash.

Wood splintered and ripped. The window banged open. All clamor by the back door ceased.

"Lowry, no!" Mandy shrilled.

Johnny heard the family stampede toward him, but they were too late. Lowry and Sam slithered out the window. He saw them skid on the wet grass before the darkness swallowed them whole.

Chapter 12

JOHNNY

JOHNNY DIDN'T HESITATE. He ducked under the sash and straddled the windowsill, but his shirttail snagged. Somebody hauled him backward with surprising strength.

Father.

"No! Stay inside!" Father bellowed. He slammed the window shut.

Sporadic shots sounded. Johnny led the charge to the upstairs window that overlooked the peach orchard and the barn. He passed the girls just outside the front room door. They clung to each other in shock as they prayed.

Johnny leaned against the window and shaded his eyes—nothing. He scrubbed at the glass with his sleeve, but it wasn't steam that obscured his vision; it was more like a drift of smoke. He focused on an orange glimmer, glad he could at least see *something*, but then his mouth went dry. He whispered, "Fire."

For a moment, his boots were nailed to the floor. All he could do was yell, "Father!" Then he unlocked his knees and ran straight into Father as he dashed downstairs. "The barn's on fire!"

Pain etched Father's face. "What else?" He gritted his teeth. "Let's go, Johnny."

But when they reached the door by the landing, there stood Mother, her arms crossed. "No, John! *You will not go out.* Why do you think they set the barn on fire? Those murderers want to draw you outside so they can kill you!"

"Don't be foolish, Jean," Father snapped. "They won't stop with me. If I don't go out there, they'll set the house afire and get rid of us all."

All of us? Why?

Father had maintained years ago, when Eliza first crossed the ice, that Biggerman would kill them all for the sheer pleasure of it. To hear someone say the words was one thing; to have somebody shoot a brother and burn down the house was another.

"Biggerman won't have to set the house on fire if the wind picks up," he said slowly. "A stray spark will do the trick."

Father and Mother stared at Johnny and fell silent.

Julia burst into the room, still holding the candle. Johnny doubted she knew it was in her hand; he took it from her and set it aside. "I think the fire is out now," she told Father. "Maybe it was too wet to burn."

"Listen!" Johnny held up a hand. Frantic barks told the tale. Cutie, Dixie, and Brownie, the Rankin dogs, had joined the battle in the peach orchard. Gunfire was replaced by shouts and growls.

"John! Jean!" A familiar voice cut through the din. "It's Bob Patton!"

Father shouted, "We're here! Thank God you've come!"

"Not just me." Even in the presence of danger, Jolly Bob rumbled out a triumphant chuckle. "I've got Hayden Thompson and our boys with me. Sit tight for a bit. We'll take care of those roughs for you."

"Much obliged, Patton! My sons"—Father's voice cracked—"that is, some of my sons may still be out there. Have a care."

A commotion ensued. Johnny was at the window in an instant. He saw a knot of villagers star-spangled with the light of their punched-tin lanterns.

"Hold your fire!" Patton shouted. "It's Sam . . . and Lowry! They're all right!"

Mandy wrenched the door open before Father thought to

protest; her joy was a sight to see. She skimmed like a swallow to Lowry's side and flung herself into his arms. Lowry tried to wrap her in his jacket, but she would not let go of him.

Then the whole house emptied into the back yard, where only hours before Johnny had watched whip-poor-wills in flight. Now the acrid smell of fire and gunpowder bit at his nostrils.

A tail thumped Johnny's leg. Cutie panted at his knee, a swatch of cloth impaled on one of her teeth. He held her gray muzzle and lifted the fabric from her fang. She washed his face with her tongue, like she already knew she was a good dog. He said it anyway and scratched behind her ear.

He handed the cloth to Father, who fingered it absently and shoved it deep into his pocket. His attention was on Lowry and Sam. "What happened?"

"There's not much to tell." Lowry shrugged it off. "We heard the shots and took off for the orchard, but Sam noticed the fire and the horses squealing. A breeze picked up sparks and blew them right toward the house."

Sam cut in. "So we ran ahead to the well house. We hauled up water and lugged it to the barn, but that's a mighty slow way to put out a fire." He smothered a cough with his sleeve, and Lowry continued.

"They'd heaped scrap wood against the barn, and it popped and sparked. The barn wall was smoking, too, like the whole thing was about to go up any minute—the harvest, the livestock, everything. I tried to scatter it, but we needed more water quick." Lowry rubbed his sooty face.

Johnny wished he'd been there. "What did you do?"

"Sam yelled, 'The trough!' So we both dipped water out and threw it on the fire, and that turned the tables."

"We smothered the ashes with earth, too," Sam told Father. "There's not too much damage done, just some scorched boards. It's a blessing that the rain dampened the wood earlier."

"Looked like it was burning pretty good to me," Lowry retorted.

Cutie sneezed. She tested the air, yipped once, and lolloped toward the cornfield. No telling whether she smelled trouble or if she was just running a raccoon out of the corn.

"Did you boys see Cal or your cousin?"

Lowry shifted his weight and Sam stared at the ground. "No, Mother."

Robert Patton cleared his throat. "Well, boys, let's split up and—"

"There's J.P.!" Johnny saw his cousin hobble from behind the smoky barn. Robert Patton reached him first. When J.P. gestured at his feet, the big man carried him pickaback to the porch.

"Got cut up pretty bad." Patton deposited him in a chair. "Why in thunder didn't you boys wear shoes?"

J.P. winced. "Is Cal back?"

"Only Lowry and Sam are here so far," Father said. "What happened?"

"I don't want to talk about it." J.P.'s bottom lip stuck out like he was going to cry.

Father threw up his hands, but Mother shook her head at him. She finished her inspection and sighed. "Mercy on us, you've cut your feet to pieces, running around barefooted like that."

"We didn't want you to hear us go out, Aunt Jean." J.P.'s expression was sheepish. "We . . . I thought you might stop us."

"You thought right." Father thundered like he was cranking up for a sermon; but to Johnny's surprise, he did a double take and sprinted for the cornfield.

And then Johnny saw Cal. His brother limped toward them with one hand on Cutie's back. Father embraced Cal and supported his weight as they rejoined the family.

Cal's shirt was black with blood. Mother exclaimed aloud and reached to touch the wound, but Cal stopped her.

"I'm all right, Mother. My feet hurt the most."

"But, Cal! You've been shot, son. Look here!" She pressed his collarbone to stanch the bleeding, but she frowned. Then she did a curious thing. Johnny watched her poke a finger right into the grisly blackness. She drew it back and rubbed the dark smear between her finger and thumb. "Why, it looks like ashes!"

"That's all it is." Cal gave a tired grin. "J.P.—is he here? Am I glad to see you!" He continued, "We split up as soon as we left the house—I went east toward the woods and he headed west toward the barn. When I came around the corner, I heard a gasp."

"Was it Biggerman?" Johnny dreaded the answer, but he had to know.

"No, it was Jairus Shoup, and we were eyeball to eyeball. I yelled. He fired point blank. I fired a shot to warn J.P., but I heard two more shots right away, and a scream." He told J.P., "I thought you were done for."

J.P. only chewed the inside of his cheek, so Cal went on, "My shoulder stung like anything, but all I could see was flashes. Finally my vision cleared, and would you believe it? My shirt was on fire. I slapped the flames out pretty quick, and that was that. He shot clear through the fabric. See, Mother?" He stuck his finger through the frayed edges of the hole and it emerged through a second hole in the back. "The bullet didn't touch me."

They marveled at the miracle, but at last Hayden Thompson asked what Johnny was wondering. "What about the other men?"

Cal glanced at J.P. "Well, my first shot went straight up, so I know I didn't hit Shoup. I don't know who all was in the peach orchard, but I don't think we did any damage there, except maybe to the trees."

"I hit Ben Mitchell." J.P. shocked them all with the force of his words.

"You mean you had a fistfight with him?" Father asked.

J.P.'s face was chalky white. He said in a strangled voice, "No, sir, I mean I shot him. I-I'm sorry." He rocked on his feet and pitched forward into Father's arms.

It seemed like forever that Father stared down at the unconscious boy. Then he said, "Help me, boys." Lowry and Sam extricated J.P. from Father's arms and carried him inside the house. Father turned a haggard face to Robert Patton. "Thanks for coming up, Bob."

"What say we do a little reconnoitering, John? Make sure they're gone." Patton spoke for the group. "You've been through enough tonight."

"I'm obliged," Father sighed. "I don't have the heart for it."

The younger boys peppered Lowry, Cal, and Sam with questions, but Mother sent them to bed. Johnny slipped out to the porch and hunched in the shadows.

He wasn't alone long before a spear of light stabbed the darkness. "Johnny!" Father shouted.

"Right here, Father."

"Thank the good Lord you did not go with Bob Patton! What are you doing out here by yourself?"

"Nothing. Father?" He spoke so quietly that Father leaned down to hear.

"What is it, Johnny?"

"Are we really doing right?"

Father stroked the top of Johnny's head. "Yes, son."

He was as rock-solid sure as ever, but Johnny wasn't. "Then why is it so hard?" The words rushed out. "We don't talk about the Underground, but everyone knows about it anyway. We didn't shoot first, but we were still attacked. We help slaves to freedom, and people hate us for it." His throat tightened and he winked away a tear.

"Not all of them, Johnny. Good friends came to our aid tonight."

"But they're our friends! They *have* to help us!"

"You're wrong, son. No one has to help us, and we don't have to help anyone. But when I think of all the suffering people just across the river, well, my course is clear." Father thought for a moment. "'Inasmuch as ye have done it unto one of the least of these my brethren, ye have done it unto me.'"

"I know that verse. *I* know why we do it." There was an embarrassing catch in Johnny's throat.

"Well, what is it, then?"

Johnny's hands flopped to his lap. "For a long time, I thought that if I told people what we do, we'd be heroes. I know better now." His sigh was shuddery with emotion. "Now all I wish is that people understood how hard it is to do right."

Father pressed Johnny's head to his side. "Stay the course, Johnny. God will take care of the rest. Don't lose heart, son."

If Father guessed that Johnny already had lost heart, he gave no sign. He pulled Johnny to his feet and they went into the house together.

⌒

Two peaceful days passed. On the third day, Johnny rode Old Sorrel through milkweed as high as his withers. A monarch butterfly rested briefly on the pommel of the saddle before flitting back to sip from the pink flowers, but Johnny didn't stop to watch. Arch Hopkins was waiting on his newspaper.

Before Johnny reached the porch, Mr. Hopkins stuck his head out the window by the door. His eyebrows drew together. "Got my paper?"

"Yes, sir. *Ripley Telegraph*." Johnny handed it over.

"Obliged," Mr. Hopkins grunted. He licked his thumb and turned the page.

"Can I talk to Eliza?"

"'Liza! Johnny Rankin's here!" Mr. Hopkins called, and he disappeared back into the house like a turtle into its shell.

When she nudged the door open, Eliza's face shone. She gripped the corners of an apron filled with ears of corn, but she transferred both corners to one hand and gave him a quick hug.

"Haven't heard from Gil yet," he told her right away. He slicked back the lank hair that flopped over his eyes and muttered, "Mr. Hopkins sure doesn't like me much."

Eliza snorted and sat down. She held the slops bucket between her knees and stripped away green shucks and corn silk with a practiced hand. "He don't like nobody 'cept Pastor Gilliland."

They grinned conspiratorially at each other.

The porch groaned as Mr. Hopkins limped out with the paper folded open. "It's cooler out here. Believe I'll join you and keep an eye on 'Liza."

She shot Johnny a wry look.

The newspaper rustled. "Your father's got a letter in here, Johnny."

"Yes, sir. What'd he say this time?"

Mr. Hopkins was pleased as Punch. "My, that man can speak his mind. There ain't no doubt about what the Reverend Rankin thinks."

The newspaper rattled as Mr. Hopkins held it at arm's length. He tilted his head and found the spot where he'd left off reading. "Says here, 'Thus have I been attacked at midnight with fire and weapons of death, and nothing but the good providence of God has preserved my property from flames and myself and my family from violence and death. And why? Have I wronged anyone? No, but I am an ABOLITIONIST.'" Mr. Hopkins interjected, "Tut, tut! You can't argue with that!"

The corner of Johnny's mouth twitched. "You'd best never try to argue with Father. He's always right."

"Well, I like a man who knows his mind, 'ceptin' when he don't agree with me." He jabbed at his spectacles with a forefinger, leaned against a post to spare his hip, and resumed reading. His lips moved silently for a while. "Listen to this! 'I do not recognize the slaveholder's right to the flesh and blood and souls of men and women.'"

"Amen," Eliza whispered.

Mr. Hopkins lapsed into silence again and Johnny thought about Eliza. She had told him a little bit about her life—the never-ending labor, the cruelty, the physical hunger, and the hunger in her soul for the Lord.

The worst part was the separation of Eliza's family. Eliza talked about her grandbabies like she'd last seen them yesterday instead of three years ago. She called them by their pet names: Essie, Shad, Mary, Meesh, and Abe. Johnny recognized the good strong Bible names; Essie was short for Esther, of course. Once he figured out that Shad was really Shadrach, the other two boys' full names were easy to guess. For three years, Eliza had prayed for them and worked for the day they could be together again. After the midnight attack, Johnny wondered if that prayer would ever be answered.

He wrenched his attention back to Father's letter, which Mr. Hopkins was still reading aloud. "'Now I desire all men to know that I am not to be deterred by fire and sword from what I believe to be my duty. I also wish all to know that I feel it is my duty to defend my HOME to the very uttermost and that it is as much a duty to shoot the midnight assassin in his attacks as it is to pray.

"'I therefore forewarn all persons to beware lurking about my house and barn at night. When I am put upon the necessity of standing guard over my family and property, I shall not do it in vain.'" Mr. Hopkins stared across the yard, lost in thought.

"He meant what he said." Johnny scratched a mosquito bite.

"Did you know that my cousin J.P. thinks he wounded Ben Mitchell? Of course," he added, "Ben fired at him first; that was the rule."

Neither one answered. Eliza glanced at Mr. Hopkins.

"What's the matter?"

Mr. Hopkins sighed. "The boy may as well know. My sons say the news is all over town."

"What news?"

Mr. Hopkins rolled the paper against his knee, his eyes glued to a spot on the post. *Smack!* He swatted a wasp. The squashed insect drifted to the porch and Mr. Hopkins flicked it into the long grass. He said, "Mitchell's dead."

Johnny stared. "I don't believe you."

"Don't matter whether you do or you don't; it's the truth, and good riddance to bad rubbish." He softened his tone. "Harriet's got your father's horse all fixed up with a switch for a tail. Why don't you take him with you and head on home?"

By the time Johnny had ridden back through the woods, cared for the horses, and turned them out, the dinner bell clanged. He brought up a pail of water and trudged to the back door, where he tipped the pail into the washbasin. Some water sloshed out over the sides—it always did.

Johnny scrubbed his hands and wiped them on his trouser legs. When he turned to go in the house, Gil was right beside him. Johnny caught his breath and held a hand to his heart.

"May I join you for . . ." The Frenchman paused to choose the right word. "Is it dinner at noon, or supper? I can never remember."

"Dinner." Johnny's heart pounded like the hooves of a runaway horse.

"Dinner, yes, thank you. I have a matter to discuss with your father."

Johnny fiddled with Mandy's bit of hair ribbon, frayed now

but still always in his pocket. What did Gil's request mean for Eliza? He nodded and stood back to let the Frenchman pass.

Dinner was unusually quiet. J.P. had been so upset when he heard the news about Ben Mitchell that he'd gone straight to bed in the middle of the day. Gil did most of the talking.

"Mr. Rankin, certainly I have found the right—gal? Gal, yes. I have worked near the Adkins place in Germantown for two months, chopping wood and clearing land, and I know it is she." He speared a pork chop and rolled some new potatoes onto his plate.

"Please have some corn, Gil." Mother passed her prettiest flowered bowl.

The Frenchman helped himself and sawed at his pork chop.

The silence did not suit Johnny; it gave him too much opportunity to think. "I guess it won't be long now until Eliza goes home with her family."

"You say it right, Johnny. It won't be long. It will be tonight."

"Now just a minute, sir." Father was beet-red. "We can't—"

"Mr. Rankin, we must." Gil buttered his bread with great deliberation. "The . . . gal, she does not have five children. She has seven."

"*What?*" Father thundered. "Eliza told me—"

"John, please. Let Gil speak," Mother interrupted.

"Thank you, Madame." He gave her a melting look. "As I say, she has seven children now. Girl, boy, girl, two boys the same, a boy, a girl." Gil shrugged. "You forget, Mr. Rankin, three years have passed."

"Seven children, all to be smuggled eight miles through the woods?" Father crossed his arms. "Impossible!"

"I did not say there would be seven to transport; there will only be six. The oldest girl, she sleeps in the plantation house, in the same room as the master and his wife. She cannot be gotten away," Gil stated flatly.

Mother gasped. "Oh, the poor lamb! Poor Eliza!"

"Although I suppose you *could* say there are seven children, if you count the one prospective." He speared a new potato, popped it into his mouth, and chewed rapturously. "Mrs. Rankin, I say it again. You are an excellent cook."

"Thank you, Gil," Mother replied. She blinked as his full meaning registered. With fingertips to her cheek, she asked weakly, "Did you say 'one prospective'? Are you sure?"

Johnny piped up. "That can't be right. Eliza told me that Beulah's husband ran off ages ago."

No one would meet his eye except Gil, and he read extreme contempt for the situation in the Frenchman's expression. He felt young and naïve when the painful truth about Beulah's condition dawned on him.

Gil replied, "Oh, yes, ma'am, very sure. Another child any moment."

"Any day, do you mean, Gil?" Mother clutched at a slim hope he'd mixed up his English vocabulary.

"I mean any moment. That is why it must be tonight." He slapped the back of his hand to his palm.

Johnny saw Mother close her eyes. "Well, there is no help for it, John. Tonight."

"But—"

"Yes." Gil rolled the word on his tongue and savored his authority. "And the old gal, Eliza, she must go along with me. I will need her help."

For the first time Johnny could recall, words failed Father.

The remaining daylight hours passed in a feverish whirl of secret messages and plans. Father himself rode over to confer with Arch Hopkins. He returned shortly before dusk and summoned Johnny and Sam. "Eliza knows you two best. Please saddle three horses."

"Shall I put the sidesaddle on Old Sorrel for her, Father?" Sam asked.

"What?" Father paused, confused. "No, use mine." He wrung his hands and darted into the house.

When they reached the barn, Old Sorrel nuzzled Sam for sugar. For once, Sam was too distracted to pay attention.

"How can she ride astride? Her legs will show," he hissed. Johnny had no answer for him as they thumbed the bits into the horses' mouths and tightened the cinches.

The boys rode up to the back porch in a daze. They leaned to kiss Mother good-bye as Father fussed over his instructions. Two spots of red still mottled his cheeks.

"Take Eliza to the lower landing. It is quieter there, and you will be less likely to be seen. Gil will be waiting with Tom Collins's skiff. Make sure Eliza brings her payment for that fellow. The sooner we get shut of this business, the better." He wrung his hands again.

Mother patted Father's arm. "They will be many miles from here by tomorrow night."

That's when it hit Johnny—Eliza was leaving. He might never see her again.

He wheeled his horse to follow Sam through the yard to the cornfield. An early spray of stars glimmered through the tall cornstalks, but the dark woods reminded Johnny of a nightmare. He imagined eyes peering at his back, but no matter how he strained his ears, he heard only their own horses. He was relieved when Mr. Hopkins hailed them.

"Sit tight, boys. I'll be back in two shakes of a lamb's tail." True to his word, he reappeared almost that fast, but with a man dressed in a familiar shad-bellied coat and slouch hat. Johnny shot a glance at Sam. Father had not mentioned Deacon Humphries. Why was Ibby's father-in-law here?

Humphries's pants flapped around his ankles, but even his cutaway coat was hard-pressed to accommodate the deacon's girth. It looked to Johnny like he'd been on an even better pasture than usual.

Then Mr. Hopkins and Deacon Humphries were beside them. Johnny looked past them. Eliza was nowhere to be seen. His stomach lurched. Something must have gone wrong.

Deacon Humphries's deep-set eyes twinkled. "Evenin', Johnny!"

His jaw dropped. He leaned to peer under the slouch hat. Deacon Humphries's old-fashioned clothes were so distinctive that it took Johnny a moment to see that the "deacon" was really Eliza in disguise.

"Better close your mouth, Johnny. Flies are a-gettin' in." Mr. Hopkins pursed his lips. "I don't hold with a woman ridin' astraddle, but she sure don't look like no woman I ever seed. Ain't she a sight, though?"

"Wish the deacon's legs was shorter." Eliza made a wry mouth at the rolled-up trousers, but she patted the bulging vest with pride. "I got my own clothes and the pouch of gold right here."

Eliza clambered aboard Old Sorrel's broad back for the last time. She twined her fingers through his creamy mane and settled herself in Father's saddle. Her stubby legs stuck out practically at right angles.

Johnny pressed his lips together as he reined in behind her and Sam. Not even the memory of Gil in pants buttoned to his shirt compared to this picturesque sight. He dared not look at his brother. Too late—he heard a snort, but he knew it wasn't from a horse. Sam hunched over the pommel, face buried against his mount's neck.

Johnny surrendered and laughed with Sam until his sides ached. "I hope I can stick on my horse whenever I catch sight of the deacon," he wheezed.

Eliza dug a hand in her hip and turned in the saddle. "Listen here, Johnny. These here man clothes is so cozy I just might keep them."

"Deacon Humphries would have to wear your dress then, Auntie." Sam wiped his eyes, feeble with laughter.

"You boys best pull yourselves together," Mr. Hopkins cautioned. He stood at Old Sorrel's side and fooled with the girth. Then he glanced back at the house. There was no sign of Mrs. Hopkins or her constant reminders about Pastor Gilliland. Old Archie's eyebrows drew together. "Better be careful, or this here gal will mammock up the whole night's work. She's stubborn as an old nanny goat."

Eliza wagged her head at him. "You're a good man, even though you take pains to hide it. God love you, Archie."

"Get along with you," he barked, but her words kindled kindness. "Take care of yourself, 'Liza." He limped back to the house.

Eliza beamed. "Oh, I can hardly wait to see those five grandbabies again!" She gathered the reins.

"Wait!" Johnny tried to prepare her for the shock. "Gil told us that there are seven children now." He hung his head.

"Seven!" Her eyes sparkled. "Oh, praise the Lord!"

"But, Auntie!" He had to say it. "Her husband is gone."

Eliza grew quiet. "That ain't them babies' fault, Johnny," she said firmly. "Good Lord knows we all they got to love them in this world, so I love them with all my heart." She pushed up a sleeve to reveal skin as lightly golden as a biscuit. "Just like my mama loved me."

He let her words sink in for a moment. Then he smiled and touched his heels to his horse's flanks. Eliza swayed in her saddle like she sat in a sideways rocking chair, but to Johnny, she had never looked more regal.

A long bridle path led through the deep woods to Cornick's

Run. The pungent smell of weeds tickled their noses as they meandered along the creek bed to the Georgetown Road. They emerged without incident at McCague's mill yard in Ripley and kept to the creek until they reached its sheltered mouth at the Ohio.

Johnny was relieved to see that Father had set everything in motion during their absence. Gil muffled the oarlocks of Thomas Collins's skiff with a thick wrapping of rags. Somebody moved in the shadows next to Gil, and Johnny almost jumped out of his skin, but it was only Mr. Collins. *Why is he here?* The man held a finger to his lips to shush the boys and Eliza.

Johnny recalled the long-ago day when the ice had broken up practically under the Englishman's nose. He hadn't heard it because, stalwart though Mr. Collins was, he was as good as stone deaf. It was common knowledge that anyone was welcome to use his skiff. He kept it chained to a stake, but every conductor knew a length of black string connected two of the links. Untie it and the skiff was ready to go.

Right now, though, every second counted. It was almost impossible to carry on a conversation with Mr. Collins, and there was no reason for him to be here, unless he had a message for them. But no one would have chosen a deaf man as a messenger.

No one but Father.

The Englishman held up his hand. Inspired choice or no, Johnny steeled himself for the ordeal of talking quietly to someone who favored a raised voice on his best days and a shout on his worst. But for once, Mr. Collins did all the talking. "Your father wants you boys to go over with Gil and bring my skiff back," he whispered. "Gil can hide his own oars and take Jack Connaughton's skiff tomorrow night when they return. Light out now, and I'll take these horses back home for you." He tipped his hat to Eliza. "The Lord bless you and keep you, Auntie." Tears spilled from his eyes as he took the horses' reins.

Gil helped Eliza into the stern, where she fastened hungry eyes on the dim Kentucky shoreline. Johnny and Sam crowded together on the seat in the bow. Gil manned the thwart.

The skiff rode low. Gil rowed without a splash or a ripple and Johnny exchanged an admiring glance with Sam. The muffled oarlocks and Gil's expert rowing made for a silent passage. When they were nearly across, the Frenchman aimed the skiff slightly downwind of Connaughton's place. With a mighty pull at the oars, he propelled the craft so far up the bank that the scrag of the hull stuck fast in the mud.

Gil hopped out, stowed the extra pair of oars in thick brush, and helped Eliza ashore. Johnny peered through the darkness at her. She held up a hand and waved; her eyes positively glowed.

"Godspeed!" he whispered. He was too scared to say more, here on the edge of no man's land. For years, Father had warned his sons against carrying the anti-slavery battle into Kentucky, yet he'd bidden them to do exactly that tonight. Small wonder that when Sam manned the oars, he rowed for their lives.

Johnny struggled to keep the skiff's course true. The dark river curled past as they quartered across the water without dropping down the current. Before they knew it, Mr. Collin's stake loomed before them, and Johnny held the skiff while Sam tied the black string. His arms ached as he and Sam heeled it for home.

Father waited glumly at the front door. "Well?"

"She's in Kentucky," Johnny reported.

"May the good Lord be with her. I wonder if it's worth the risk to try to save the rest of her family when she is already free." Sam went in with Father, and the door clicked shut.

Johnny thought of Eliza's transfigured face just before she crossed to Kentucky. Worth it? He reckoned so.

He removed his hat and sat on the front steps while his back muscles bunched and twitched. A late firefly traced copperplate script on the air. Johnny watched it glow and fade, glow and fade, the only light visible save for the path of the young moon on the river. Wait—some flash of white down in town arrested his gaze at the same instant that a breeze ruffled his hair. The white patch flapped again; it was just Mrs. Dodds's wash. She'd left her laundry out after dark again.

He wasn't sure what he was waiting for until he heard it. The sound sent shivers up his back. He held his breath when the hound bayed again. Connaughton's Belle; no doubt about it.

Please, God. He strained his eyes but there was nothing to see.

There was nothing else to hear, either. Belle and all the other dogs remained silent. Johnny closed his eyes. *Thank You.*

His finger throbbed. Bewildered, he saw that he had wound Mandy's blue hair ribbon so tight that he'd nearly cut off the circulation. He went inside and climbed the stairs for bed.

Hours later, he awoke. Sam snored gently beside him while Johnny flexed his back.

He wondered whether Eliza and Gil had made it to Germantown. They had planned to intercept Eliza's daughter as she went out before daylight to milk the cows. Johnny imagined how he would feel if Mother had gone away for three years and suddenly reappeared.

A lump caught in his throat as he told himself the story. The daughter would stop dead in her tracks and whisper, "Mama!" as if she had seen a ghost. Eliza would kiss Beulah, and Gil would hustle them into the house. Perhaps the stoic Frenchman would dash away a tear. Johnny imagined Beulah's quiet pride as she introduced her youngest children to their grandmother, who would fling her arms wide and hold them as she had yearned to do for so long.

He yawned and stared out the window toward the first light of dawn. If only he could be there to see Eliza's prayers answered at last.

Chapter 13

ELIZA

ELIZA PLODDED BEHIND GIL. That's what he said to call him, but he flinched every time she said it. Gil. Such an outlandish name, like fish parts.

When they'd left the river, he'd whispered to her that they had eight miles to walk, as the crow flies. That was the last thing he'd said. Her body cried out that surely they had covered that distance twice by now. She puffed as she climbed the hills between her and her family. When she had left Canada, she could walk all day and not get tired. She'd gotten soft since she'd been hidden away on Old Archie's farm.

They topped another ridge as the night sky brightened a bit. Gil pointed. "That's Adkins's place."

Eliza caught her breath. The Adkins's farm lay in a hollow. She nearly pushed past Gil in her eagerness to get there, but he caught her arm. He motioned to a currant bush to the west of the tiny gray log cabin where Beulah and her seven children lived. Then he led the way down the hill. Blackberry briars tore at her hands and ankles as she charged through the brush.

The next instant, she almost jumped out of her skin as a hound dog bayed, the deep voice tolling like a bell. Gil's hand flashed to his pocket. Before Adkins's dog reached the breathless pair, the Frenchman tossed a bacon rind. The dog fawned and snatched the meat. Gil shooed the dog away, and it slunk down the hill with its prize.

When they reached the currant bushes, Gil settled in to wait. Eliza offered a quick prayer. Then she watched for Beulah.

In the chilly half-light of dawn, the landscape took shape around them. A mockingbird as gray as the morning swooped to the clothesline stretched between two trees. He fluffed his white-barred wings, threw back his head, and poured out his thanks for the new day.

The cabin door scraped and there stood Beulah, great with child. She hitched along the path with a fist balled to the small of her back. Eliza caught her breath. Gil patted the air to signal "not yet." She nodded and bit her lip until tears brimmed. Better to let her daughter milk the cows first so nothing would seem amiss.

The minutes stretched. A brown rabbit, so young that a white snip of fur was still visible between its eyes, scooted into the thicket just inches from where Gil and Eliza sat like statues. A stray shaft of sunlight slanted to illuminate translucent ears. The pink nose twitched as the baby sniffed at a patch of clover and selected a stem. The busy jaws nibbled the stem until only the pink and red blossom remained. The rabbit froze in midchew. Fringed clover bristled from its mouth like a red mustache. Paws scratched furiously at the dirt. Carefully the rabbit twisted and rolled in the loose earth, then stretched lazily on its side to finish the clover.

Eliza smiled and nudged Gil, but he only licked his lips, like he was thinking a rabbit stew would taste mighty good about now.

The sound of labored breathing alerted them. Eliza moved like lightning to a crouch. Her scratched hands parted the branches. The startled rabbit bolted, straight across Beulah's path. She started and peered nearsightedly at the bushes.

Gil whispered, "Now," and Eliza straightened, an inch at a time. Her daughter squinted and put down the pail of milk to step closer.

"Mr. Adkins, that you, sir? I just this minute finished milking," she began, but she stopped. Her eyes widened. She scrambled backward. "Who are you? What you doin' here? Don't you come sneakin' round here and try to steal me away to New Orleans!"

Eliza took an involuntary step forward and caught sight of the suit she wore. No wonder Beulah didn't recognize her own mother.

"Don't you come near me. I'll holler, do you hear? I'll holler!" She clutched her belly and opened her mouth wide.

Gil crashed out of the thicket toward the woman while she screamed like the whistle on the Ripley ferry. He choked off her wind with one hand and smothered her squeals with the other.

"Do that again and I will strangle you, understand?" he hissed. She sagged against him and nodded her head. He gave her a little shake and said, "Look!"

Eliza swept off her hat. Her lips trembled. "Beulah, child, it's Mama. I done come back for you."

Beulah stiffened; that got through. Gil relaxed his hold. She hobbled a few uncertain steps, placed her hands on Eliza's shoulders, and peered into her eyes. Eliza saw recognition flicker. Beulah shook all over. Before Gil could react, she caterwauled again, this time for pure joy.

Panic swept over Eliza. "Hush your squallin'!" she breathed. She shot a glance at the farmhouse.

Sure enough, curtains twitched and a face appeared at a window. "Beulah," a voice thick with sleep demanded, "what's all that ruckus about?"

Instantly Gil and Eliza retreated to the thicket, leaving Beulah alone in the semidarkness. "Tell him there is a snake! Be quick!"

"They's a copperhead snake out here, Mr. Adkins! I about stepped on it," she called weakly.

"Well, kill it, for pity's sake, and stop tryin' to wake the dead," he shouted.

Beulah made a beeline for the thicket before the curtains fell. Gil struck his forehead in despair and flailed both arms for her to stay away. Beulah stopped, squinted, and nodded her head. Her eyes never left the currant bushes.

Before Eliza could stop him, Gil shoved Beulah toward the big house to cook breakfast as usual. If she didn't show up soon, the whole house would be in an uproar. He told her as much and threatened to kill her if she told anyone, especially Essie, that they were there. She nodded again, and Eliza let out a grateful sigh. If there was one thing Beulah could do, it was keep her mouth shut. Eliza well-remembered her week-long sulks.

They waited until Beulah started up the path, slow as a balky mule. Then the Frenchman hustled Eliza inside the cabin.

She'd waited so long to see him, the boy who stood by the fireplace. He had grown some, but he was still almost too spindly to stir the pot full of mush suspended over the smoky fire. *Will he know me?*

"Shadrach," Eliza whispered.

The boy dropped the spoon and whirled, mouth clamped shut, but his big eyes told the tale. He barreled toward her, and she folded him in her arms. *He knows, Lord,* Eliza marveled. *This child knows I've come for him.* Gil tugged at her sleeve, but Eliza brushed him off like a gnat. She crooned, "Mammaw's come back. Mammaw's here."

Twenty kisses or so was all the time she had to get reacquainted with Shad. Gil removed the center log of the puncheon floor before Eliza could say another word. He snatched a raggedy, red quilt from right over top of the children who snored in the bedstead by the fireplace and wrapped it around her. He held her hand as she stepped into the hollowed-out place below the floor and lay down. Then he carefully replaced the yellow poplar log. The light above her dimmed and Eliza guessed that Gil had flipped a rag rug to cover the crack between the logs.

"Can you hear me?"

"Yes, sir."

"Good. I will hide until Mr. Adkins is in bed one hour tonight. You know when the whip-poor-will sings?"

"Early candlelight."

"When you hear him, be ready, and I will come. Only pack what you need for one night. This boy will pull the latchstring in and leave by the window." The board squeaked, and Eliza heard Gil speak to Shadrach. "Today, you keep everyone quiet. Mama will do her work at the big house and stay busy. Can you lift this log?" Eliza imagined Shadrach's proud nod. "Do so one hour after the lights go out in the big house. Your sister there, she cannot come with us. Do not tell her." There was a stricken silence, and when Gil spoke again, his voice was husky. "Truly, I am sorry," he said. His footsteps echoed, and he was gone.

Eliza heard Shad sniffle once, and a lump rose in her throat. She could hardly bear to leave Essie behind. She lay still, numb with grief over the loss of the girl. She lost track of how long she wept without making a sound. At long last, weariness overcame her and sleep eased her pain.

An insistent tapping awakened Eliza from her doze. Dark— where in the world was she? Gradually her eyes adjusted. Long strips of mellow light barred what felt like cloth wrapped around her. A damp smell of old clay stirred memories—some good, some nightmarish. A feathery something crept on her cheek. Her skin crawled; she hoped to goodness it was not a spider. She brushed away the feeling, her knuckles grazing roughness just above her. Under the floor, that's where she was. As far as she stretched, she touched the same uneven surface until her fingers located a slim crack where the light shone through. She squirmed toward it and saw a brown eye.

"Mammaw! Y'all's snoring! Be quiet. You hear?"

"Shad?" she whispered. The eye bobbed. "I hear," she said. Dust sifted through the crack as the rug came down.

Eliza edged back to the hollow of earth where she had lain since dawn. A scuffle of footsteps tottered across the floor. Which grandbaby would that be, she wondered? Maybe it was one she'd not yet met. She strained her ears.

"Come here, Lulie. Here's your mush," Shad coaxed. Footsteps swished. "Georgie, come on."

Fresh tears welled up when she thought of the family time stolen away. These children were strangers to her, but she was not the only one to suffer. It hurt Eliza's heart to think of Shad, who should have been out skylarking, maybe even learning to read. Instead he served as both father and mother to his younger brothers and sisters. She thought, too, of Biggerman's dead green eyes as he ogled Beulah.

She must have dozed off again because all of a sudden she saw Shad's snaggle teeth and huge smile. Carefully he set the puncheon down and reached to pull her upright. Her joints popped as she stood.

The next person she saw in the flickering candlelight was Beulah, who held a cautious hand over Lulie's and Georgie's mouths. Their round eyes raked the monster who crawled out of the floor. Eliza bided her time and turned her attention to the bigger kids. Shad fell on her neck and nearly choked the living daylights out of her. Loath to let Shad outdo them, Meesh, Abe, and Mary piled on, too, until Eliza's arms were full of sharp-elbowed, knobby-kneed children.

Someone tugged at her skirts. Lulie stood at her knee with a finger in her mouth. Corkscrew curls the color of straw strayed every which way.

"She looks just like you when you was a baby, Beulah," Eliza breathed reverently. She snuggled the older children and set them down. She held out a hand to Lulie, who batted familiar green eyes at the floor. Then the finger popped out of her mouth and she reached for Eliza, who snatched her up and kissed her. That was too much for shy Georgie. He squirmed himself into his grandmother's embrace.

"I used to call your mammy 'Lulie,'" she whispered to the little girl. To Beulah she said, "Your daddy gonna be mighty proud you named a boy after him."

The corn shuck mattress rustled as Beulah sat down and squeezed Eliza for dear life. Her mouth worked, but she could not speak. No matter. Eliza could see her daughter's soul in her eyes.

Shad piped up. "She's got all our stuff packed, Mammaw."

Eliza petted Beulah, who nodded modestly. "Then we almost ready to go. You're a good girl, honey." She spied a lumpy pile in the corner of the cabin and drew her eyebrows together. "What's all that?"

Shad sighed. "I done told you, Mammaw. She's got *all* our stuff packed up."

Eliza handed Lulie to her mother and crossed the puncheon floor. She stared at five heaps of household goods bundled up in threadbare quilts. "Beulah, child, what's all this truck?" she whispered. "Gil said pack what we need for *one day*."

"I did, Mama. This yere baby's gonna come any time. No tellin' what-all I'll need." She poked out her lower lip.

"Beulah Mae, you got three hunnerd pounds of stuff here." She prodded one of the bundles. "How'd you get a skillet? You been sneakin' stuff outen the house today?"

"No tellin' what-all I'll need," Beulah repeated doggedly. "Ooh," she clutched her belly.

Eliza tried again. "Beulah, child, we got no call to do Mr. Adkins this away. And who you think's gonna carry it all?"

"These childrens is plenty strong enough to carry these little old packs." Beulah's chin jutted.

"Why, Beulah, honey!" Eliza watched her grandbabies. Shad seemed older, but he was only seven. Mary was a year younger, and the twins, Meesh and Abe, had just turned five. Three-year-old Georgie clambered up one of the bundles and slid to the floor with a resounding thump.

A whip-poor-will called. Instantly, Shad cracked the cabin door and peeped out. Gil eased through and shut the door behind him.

"Ready?"

Shad looked at Gil in mute appeal and jerked a thumb at the mounds of plunder.

A scowl blackened the Frenchman's face. He rounded on Beulah and Eliza. "What do you mean by this? No! Leave it!"

"I need it." Beulah moaned and turned away from him. Her skirts swayed as she paced toward the pile of stuff, both fists kneading her back.

Eliza pulled Gil aside in desperation. "She's like a broody hen," she confided. "Some women's like that when their time's near—they fuss around, build a nest. We gots to coddle her."

Gil struck his palm. "It is an impossibility."

"Looky yonder," Eliza told him. They watched as Beulah tightened the knots on her bundles with fierce concentration. She did not seem to know anyone else was in the cabin. "I know my Beulah. She's balky as an old mule. She won't step foot outen this place 'lessen we promise to take it all. We gots to coddle her," she repeated.

Gil closed his eyes and muttered a steady stream of mumbo jumbo. Then he said, "It will be this way. You and I will carry the packs. *She* will look after the children. You will help her, yes, Shad?" The boy nodded. "Keep her busy, looking at the children, listening for dogs, oh, anything." Gil's expression waxed droll. "When your mama does not see, we will leave what we can behind."

Shad grinned at him, man to man.

Then Gil was everywhere, dousing candles, ransacking the beds, banking the fire so that a trickle of smoke wisped from the chimney—anything to give them a head start.

At last he was satisfied. He swung a pack to his shoulders and grunted with the effort. "Let's go."

Eliza knelt to distribute the goods more evenly in her pack. She pulled one corner high to hide her other hand while she shoved Missus Adkins's heavy skillet under the bedstead. She knotted the quilt and balanced the bundle on her head while she held Lulie on her hip.

Beulah nudged another bundle with her toe. "Now, Mama, they all gots to go. Shad, you pick up this yere bundle. Mary, here's one for you."

"Hush your frettin', gal. Those children can't even lift half what you got in here. Me and this man will carry your bundles. We'll walk a little ways and put one down, then we'll come back for another. Shad will help you mind the children."

Eliza took stock of her rag-tag band of refugees. "Somebody's gonna have to tote Georgie part ways. He's too chunky to walk far on his own. Can you do that, Shad? That's Mammaw's big boy. All right, it'll be a weary long time before our walk's over, so we all gots to help one another," she encouraged. "Wait, boys! Where's y'all's hats? Can't leave without those. There, that's better."

Gil said, "Now, Shad, we will all go out. You bar the door, pull in the latchstring, then climb out the window. We will wait for you behind the currant bush."

Soon, Shad wormed through the window. A whole flock of butterflies tickled Eliza's stomach. It was time.

A young moon lighted the way. Crickets shrilled. Stealthy rustles in the brush, a breeze that rattled through the tree-tops—Eliza had never noticed so many night sounds before, but she was thankful for anything that would blot out the sound of their passage.

Hoist a bundle, take the baby from Shad, and push on. Snatch one child out of a poison ivy patch, grit teeth while waiting on another to finish his private business, and answer, "Around the daisy!" when yet another asked where they were all going. Put down the bundle, rest the baby on top under Shad's watchful eye, backtrack, pick up another bundle, and do it all again for hours on end.

The pattern wore away the night until a mighty ridge loomed in the darkness. Gil grabbed a sapling, planted a foot, and hauled himself to a point above their heads.

Crumbles of earth and rock rolled to Eliza's feet. She gaped from Gil to Beulah.

Beulah flat-out balked. "I can't."

Gil let go and slid backward to the ground. He stood with arms akimbo and motioned with his head. "Our path lies that way."

Eliza leveled a glare at him. "You ever have a baby?"

His eyebrows jumped. "Madame," he protested.

"Then you better help me, or she ain't never gonna cross that ridge." She thrust her hands at him. He curled his lip and took hold. "Beulah, honey. Come on now," Eliza coaxed.

"I can't breathe." Beulah rested her arms over top of her head and panted.

Mary hid a smile. "Mama, you look like a puppy dog."

"Hush up, now," Eliza warned. Tears sprang into her eyes. She and Gil braced their arms behind the small of Beulah's back. Together they supported her as she inched up the ridge.

All her life, Eliza had heard far-fetched tales of settlers chocking wagon wheels with chunks of rock to keep them from rolling back down the ridges when they first came to Kentucky. She believed those stories with all her heart now, and she put them to good use. Whenever they found a sturdy tree, she and

Gil propped Beulah against it while they helped the children climb ever higher. Only three bundles of household plunder remained, but Beulah watched them like a starved cougar. Eliza chirked up to see that spunk, but it did not strike Gil the same way.

"We will never make it before dawn," he snarled as he backtracked.

"Leave that bundle lay," Eliza directed. "She's got other worries 'long about now. We can tote these last two bundles; they don't amount to much."

Only Gil noticed when they topped the ridge at last. Instead of going forward, he dropped Eliza's hands and struck off to the left.

"Where you going?"

"We follow this ridge to the river."

Eliza stilled. Sure enough, she heard the water slap the bank. The wonderful dank smell of river mud greeted her. She stepped toward it and barked her shin on a stone. A quick inspection of her leg revealed a lump that ached something fierce. Her fingers sought what she had bumped. A thin slab worn smooth tipped toward her; she must have caught an edge.

And then she knew what it was—a tombstone. She scrambled backward faster than a crawdad. Her skin crawled at the chalky feel of the stone, and she wiped her hands on her skirts. She sidled toward Gil. She had just about reached him when the ground opened to swallow her right leg up to her hip.

Eliza clawed out of the hollow grave before the children got spooked. She shook off the notion that a bony hand had raked her ankle, trying to keep her in Kentucky forever.

When they had descended the ridge, Gil fell in step beside Eliza. "We have almost reached the river. We will wade in the water to Jack Connaughton's cornfield. His farm is across the river from the Rankins'. You will hide in the corn until tonight. I will cross over and confer on what must be done. You must keep them all quiet until I come back. Do you understand?"

"Yes, sir, I surely do," Eliza answered solemnly. She pried off her shoes, tied the laces together, and tucked them in her bundle. It took a real tussle to get Beulah's shoes off. Her daughter's feet were so puffy that Eliza could hardly feel her ankle bones.

For a moment, she doubted her mission. What if something awful happened to Beulah or the baby? Likely enough, though, the cold water would take down the swelling some. With that thought, Eliza swept her doubts aside and helped the kids with their shoes. She rolled up the boys' trouser legs and her own. Then she tucked up Beulah's and Mary's skirts to keep them out of the wet.

The children had never seen a real river before, but there was no time to gawk at it now. The shallows along the shore would carry away their scents and hide their passage from the river patrollers and their sharp-nosed hounds.

When the first little foot sank into the fishy mud, though, the whole plan almost collapsed. Georgie cut loose with a howl. Faster than chain lightning, Eliza's hand zipped to her kerchief and she popped a piece of sorghum cane in his mouth. She watched his surprise as the sweet juice washed over his tongue. He chomped on it so hard he forgot all about the mud that smeared his chubby legs up to the knees. Gil almost smiled as Eliza produced pieces for all the other children except Lulie, who slumbered on her shoulder.

When it was barely daylight, Gil stopped so fast that Shad bumped smack into him and sat down in the river with a splash. "We must take cover." He pointed to a trickle of water that emptied into the Ohio from between two rugged hills. "That's Boland's Gut. Keep to the water." He followed the gut upstream, and Eliza had to hustle to keep up.

Almost immediately, Mary slipped when a rock teetered under

her foot. Meesh thought he saw a snake slither out from under the rock. Eliza bent over to peer at what *looked* like a stubby snake. She petted Meesh's head. "Shucks, that's just a little old mud puppy salamander. He won't hurt you none."

Presently they came to a clearing where Gil parted cornstalks higher than his head. He walked deep into the cornfield with the little flock trailing behind him. After a mighty long way, he eased his bundle to the ground. Beulah groaned and sank to lean against the pack. She fell asleep instantly, her arm curled over the plunder.

The Frenchman approached Eliza, strangely humble. "You must stay here until late tonight. The water . . . branch? The branch is just behind if you need water. I will come back for you. Don't be afraid. I think—" Gil paused. "I think your God is with you. In fact, I am certain of it." He took Eliza's roughened hand in his, kissed it, and he was gone.

Eliza wasted no time getting settled. She worked at the knot of the pack she had toted for miles. She eased the quilt open and shook her head over the useless items Beulah had packed. Her eyes widened when she saw the drinking gourd. She waved it at Shad and whispered, "Crawl over to that branch yonder and bring back some water for us, little man."

She looked at the other children. Lulie had curled up on her mama's skirts and was sleeping like an angel, but Meesh, Abe, Mary, and Georgie's stomachs growled.

Eliza rooted through the pack but found not a scrap of food. The children watched her like a nestful of baby robins. *Well, this is a fine thing. All these hungry babies to feed and nothing but corn as far as I can see.*

She rubbed her chin and gazed at the walls of corn. *Raccoons gobble corn raw,* she mused. *Why not people?*

"Lord, bless our food. Amen." Quick as she shucked one ear, an eager hand grabbed it, and the children wolfed down the blister corn. Shad returned several times with water. They slurped gratefully, Eliza last of all. She smoothed out a quilt between the furrows and patted it to show they should rest. *Sleeping children are quiet children.* The young ones soon dropped off to sleep, milky kernels still pasted to their lips.

Now only Shad and Eliza remained alert as the sun climbed in the sky. Shad drowsed in the warmth. His muddy legs jerked, and he woke up. Eliza put her whole heart into a smile and beckoned for him to lie down. He shook his head and stifled a yawn.

"Sleep now," she whispered. "We need a rested man later." With a proud, bleary grin, Shad stretched out and slept in the waving shade of the cornstalks.

Eliza settled down to wait for Gil.

Chapter 14

JOHNNY

"CAUTION AND VIGILANCE are of the utmost importance. We must go on with our daily work."

Johnny sopped his biscuit in warm, yellow egg as Father outlined the plan for the day. He forked another crisply browned egg.

"You cultivate the corn, Johnny. It's getting away from us again."

Johnny nodded and savored each bite. Mother fried her eggs in bacon grease, and he could never get enough of the smoky sweet flavor. He nestled a few more slices next to the eggs on his plate and dribbled honey over another buttery biscuit.

The long list of chores complete, Father moved on. "As for vigilance . . ."

A knock at the door saved Johnny from hearing what he could recite as well as Father. He split a biscuit and stuck two pieces of bacon in the middle to tide him over on the way to the back door.

The youngest Collins boy stood on the back porch, shifting from one foot to the other. When Johnny opened the door, the boy fished a scrap of paper from his vest pocket. "This is for your papa."

Johnny fixed a serious expression on the lad. "What's it say?"

The boy shrugged. "I don't know how to read yet." He jumped off the back porch.

Johnny chuckled; the answer never varied. Caution and vigilance demanded a messenger too young to know his letters. "Wait a minute!" He dashed back to the table for one of Mother's tender doughnuts. The boy's face lit up. "Here you go. Careful going home."

Johnny ran the edge of the note under his fingernail. *Almost time now.* Eliza must be nearly beside herself with joy.

"At last," Father said when Johnny gave him the message. He braced his elbow on the back of his chair and propped up a foot. The cheerful clamor of breakfast continued as Father scanned the note, raised the stove lid, and pitched the scrap into the fire.

"They didn't make it." He stared into the flames.

The sudden silence rang in Johnny's ears until his scalp prickled. "What?"

But Father was halfway out of the room already. "Cal, make sure all the work goes on as usual. Sam, Johnny, let's go."

Johnny drained his milk and swung his legs over the bench at the same time everyone else tried to leave the table. For a moment, confusion reigned.

"Boys!" Mother forced a halt. "John. Is Eliza all right?"

Father spread his hands and shook his head. "Pray," he said. Johnny followed him and Sam out the door.

The three of them split up when they reached the edge of town. Johnny headed south on Mulberry Street. He pulled his hat low and strolled to Mr. Collins's cabinet shop. He knocked twice and entered, galloped past the raw pine coffins, and took the stairs two at a time.

Gil sat in the upstairs office, but he bore little resemblance to the jocular Frenchman who had so adroitly rowed Eliza across the Ohio River. Crusty eyes and rumpled hair and clothing bespoke a sleepless night.

Sam wedged in behind Johnny; the room was crowded with

nervous abolitionists. By the time Father joined Mr. Collins, Mr. McCague, Deacon Humphries, and burly Robert Patton, it was difficult to breathe in the tiny room. Mr. Collins locked the door behind Patton and drew the curtains.

"What happened?" Father demanded.

"Monsieur Rankin," Gil protested.

Father held up a hand. "First things first. Is Eliza all right?"

"I believe her to be so. They are hidden in Connaughton's cornfield."

Father blanched. "Why, I can see that place from here. Do you mean to say those women will have to stay there all day with six small children?"

Gil regarded him with a cold stare before he responded. "The gal, she packed three hundred pounds of stuff." He shrugged. "The old woman said we must—coddle? Yes, coddle her, because her time is near. We carried forward, set down, walked back, carried forward, set down—across eight miles of hollows and timber. We kept track of six children and rested whenever the gal so much as groaned. We walked in the water to throw off the dogs. I should like to see anyone in this room do better."

He waited; there were no takers.

"What now?" Mr. Collins cupped a hand to his ear and waited.

"I left Connaughton's skiff in plain view on this side of the river. I believe the patrollers will come over here immediately to search. That may serve to keep the old gal safe for a while."

A general murmur of assent mollified the Frenchman.

"I will go over tonight when the patrollers have passed by. When the dogs bark no more, I will know it is time, yes? I will bring them back—where?"

"To my house." Thomas McCague raised his head from his hands. "Kittie and I have that third-story room, plenty big enough for them all. I leave it to you gentlemen how we will proceed after that, but bring them to my house tonight." He stared into space. "We have entertained so many of our Kentucky friends there." His voice broke. "Maybe they won't think of searching our home."

"Well, that's settled," Father said. "We've tarried long enough. Everyone must go about his business. We'll do some planning today and reconvene tomorrow morning. Come, boys."

"There is one detail you have forgotten, sir."

Every eye turned to the Frenchman.

"Why, what can that be?" Father asked in amazement.

"Forgive me, sir, but I think the old gal would count it as a favor if you were to pray for her. She was already praying as I left. Almost—almost, she persuades me to trust in God as she does."

Johnny paused with his hand on the key. He saw every man in the room bow his head. He closed his eyes, too.

"Dear Lord, we ask for your guidance and protection. Shelter Eliza and her family and keep them safe. In Jesus' name we pray, Amen." A tinge of color had returned to Father's pale cheeks as he dismissed them. "Meet here before church. See you at the house, boys."

Saturday dragged its heels. Johnny fretted over Eliza while he cultivated corn, while he salvaged windfall peaches from the orchard, and while he drove home the cows for his sisters to milk. If he managed to forget the danger, one glance toward Kentucky brought it home. Connaughton's cornfield—he could practically reach out and touch it.

He wandered to his hedge apple tree. The graceful arch of branches blotted Kentucky from sight as he stepped over exposed orange roots to lean against the trunk. He retrieved Mandy's ribbon from his pocket, threaded it in and out over his knuckles, and pulled the smoothness through his fingers.

I'm sorry, Lord.

That very moment, he knew God had heard him. The good

Lord lifted the heavy burden of guilt about the secret he'd had no right to share, no matter what the circumstances. All that mattered now was that he, his family, and Eliza trusted in God. What had they to fear?

Johnny woke up before the chickens the next morning, his heart light with gratitude. In just a few hours Eliza would be with her family, the dear ones she longed to deliver to freedom.

"Savior, like a shepherd lead us," he sang. He brought in a pail of water to drink with the cold breakfast his family ate on Sunday mornings. "Blessed Jesus, blessed Jesus . . ." Almost dawn—Father and Sam would have to hustle if they were going make it down to Mr. Collins's shop before church.

Somewhere outside, Cutie whined. Johnny wandered to the front window, where the gray light softened the familiar river scene to indistinct smears. He stepped outside with a fragrant peach and leaned to take a bite, careful not to let the sweet juice dribble on his Sunday clothes. Wood smoke from several chimneys drifted up the hill; his eyes smarted.

Cutie nudged his hand, and he ruffled her ears. She leaned against his leg and returned to her vigil.

Johnny gobbled the rest of the peach and set the fresh stone on the window ledge. He tested the stone he'd left there the other day—dry. He dropped it into his pocket as he slurped peach juice from his fingers.

A breeze meandered through the tall grass like it was lost. Cutie devoutly sorted one wind-borne scent from another and perked her ears.

"Smell a rabbit over there, girl?"

She whined again and shaped her mouth to bark but snapped her jaws shut instead. Johnny frowned.

Then the sun crested a purple cloud, and the indistinct smears on the Kentucky hillside came into focus. At least thirty mounted men swarmed the Connaughton place. A pack of hounds boiled over each other in their eagerness to be released into the corn.

A sob wrenched loose from deep inside Johnny's throat. So the Frenchman's ruse had not worked—it was all over for Eliza. The soles of his boots were rooted to the spot as he stared at the awful spectacle across the river.

Father spoke from somewhere behind him. "It's too late to go down to Tom's place. We'll go to Sunday school as we always do."

Wind cooled the sweat on Johnny's forehead. "You think she made it across?"

Father shaded his eyes. "Looks like they're still searching, so there's hope. But even if she did make it, Johnny, those roughs will soon follow, and they'll pay volunteers to search for her, just as they always do, with the promise of plenty of whiskey to boot. But before that, they'll have to ride downriver a few miles to the Augusta ferry." He jabbed his walking stick first to the right and swung it in a wide arc to the left. "Or upriver a ways to the one in Maysville. That'll take a while."

Johnny's throat constricted. "Eliza is my friend."

"Yes, that makes it harder."

"You don't understand. I—I told Mrs. Stowe all about her when I was at Lane. I wanted to be a hero. She promised not to tell, but what if she did?" His confession came out in a rush.

Father's hand rested on his shoulder. "Have you talked to the Lord about it?"

He nodded.

"Then rest in the assurance that 'all things work together for good to them that love God.' Let Him handle it. Don't be afraid, son."

Don't be afraid. He repeated the words to himself a hundred times before Sunday school ended. When it was time for the service, Johnny watched his family file into their accustomed spots in the sanctuary, some in the choir with him and some in the family pew. Most Sundays he looked forward to the piano music before the service. Today, the notes jangled his soul. He fingered Mandy's frayed hair ribbon and chewed his lip as the seconds crawled.

When the choir finished the anthem and took their seats, Johnny hoped he'd sung in tune. His gaze lighted on Mother—not a trace of worry to be seen. He wished his own faith were as strong as hers. How much better he would feel if Thomas and Kittie McCague went to Father's church! Then he could ask them what happened and lay his worries about Eliza to rest.

Father opened his Bible with a resounding thump. "Today's text is taken from the one hundred and fourth Psalm."

Relief washed over Johnny in waves; he was so glad to have something else to think about. He settled down to concentrate on the message.

"'Bless the LORD, O my soul . . .'" The familiar verses comforted Johnny as Father read them through. "'He sendeth the springs into the valleys, which run among the hills. They give drink to every beast of the field. . . . He causeth the grass to grow for the cattle, and herb for the service of man. . . . The sun ariseth, they gather themselves together, and lay them down . . . let the wicked be no more. Bless thou the LORD, O my soul. Praise ye the LORD.'"

After the prayer for guidance, Father began the sermon. "When I was a young boy in Tennessee," he said, "I was accustomed to working hard. If we needed shoes to wear, why, we must raise and kill a beef. We preserved half and took half to a tanner. The tanner cured the hide for us and took the beef in payment. Then we took the hide home and worked it into harness or shoe leather. When I was a bit older, I made my wedding shoes with my own hands." He displayed his calloused palms to the congregation. "We had what we needed, but we had to work hard to get it. We did not depend on another to do our work for us."

An uncomfortable rustle arose from Mother's pew. Johnny watched Father's color rise as he warmed to his story.

"There was a certain man in the vicinity, however, who did no honest work. Occasionally, he would sell his household goods to buy whiskey. When the clamoring of his hungry children became too much to bear, that's when this lazy man went to work at last. And once, I had the misfortune to witness this man's method of providing for his family. I was just a shy boy of seven when I heard a noise as I picked apples."

Johnny automatically looked for Lowry as he always did when Father mentioned shyness, but Lowry's place was empty—he'd gone to Cincinnati for an appointment with the district officers of the church.

"I stood very still on my ladder amidst the branches and peeped. On the other side of the fence near our hen house, very near to me, I saw this certain man. He had a nail and a few kernels of corn. He used the nail and a rock to pierce one kernel. Then he took a long, heavy piece of string and passed it through the hole. He tied the two ends of the string together in a knot. Then he stretched out on his stomach behind some brush and tossed the kernel of corn into the middle of my vegetable garden, where my mother's fat hens scratched."

An appreciative chuckle rippled through the congregation, but Johnny glanced Mother's way and caught the tail end of a scowl. He had to admit this was nothing like Father's usual sermons.

"Well, in no time, a hen gobbled up that piece of corn, and the thief reeled in my mother's hen, just as if it were a fish. The hen strangled and carried on until the old rooster raised a ruckus, but I did not say a word when the thief tucked the hen under his arm and ran. I knew the man's children, knew how starved and helpless they were."

Father held up an admonishing finger. "Now, we could ill afford the loss of that one hen, for we ate some of her eggs, sold others for egg money, set her on some eggs to hatch baby chicks into more laying hens, and when she was old, tough, and no longer laying, we would have enjoyed a supper of my mother's stewed chicken and dumplings. So for our neighbor to steal our hen, that was certainly a low-down crime. For a time, I thought no one could sink lower."

Father paused again and his gaze roamed the sanctuary. His cheeks flushed. "But now I've seen a crime that is even lower than stealing hens."

Johnny straightened up in his pew and craned at Mother. She directed the barest shake of her head at Father. He ignored her.

"There are men in Ripley who hire out for a dollar a day to chase helpless runaway slaves and return them to their masters. Mark that—a dollar a day. Make no mistake, friends." Father's Sunday voice soared to ping off the rafters; surely even the slave hunters over in Kentucky could hear him as he wound up and let the words fly. He stabbed the air with an upraised finger. "I would rob a hen roost myself before I would deliver a runaway slave back to his master." The words sank like stones into the pool of silence.

Mother shook her head openly, but Father was not finished. "Hear now the words of King David: 'The LORD that delivered me out of the paw of the lion, and out of the paw of the bear, he will deliver me out of the hand of this Philistine.'"

Father allowed the message to register a moment with his flock before he launched into the familiar parable of Lazarus and the rich man, but Johnny's thoughts lagged far behind. He saw a mere shepherd boy armed with only a sling and five smooth stones as he advanced to do battle with a giant.

The rest of the service was slow torture. In his mind's eye, Johnny saw relentless bloodhounds in pursuit of his friend and her family. He saw Eliza, her face raw with grief, as Laban Biggerman ripped away her daughter and grandbabies for the second time in her life. He saw her heavy shackles drag as she boarded the slave boat bound for New Orleans. He saw her lying in a cotton field, beaten senseless.

By the time the two-hour church service ended, Mandy's hair ribbon was in shreds and Johnny's insides had turned to water. He trudged out of the sanctuary dead last and joined his family.

Mother and Father had taken Sunday dinner at the McCague house for almost twenty years, but they made no pretense of going there today. The streets of Ripley fairly hummed with activity. A crowd of strange men milled outside every tavern; their bleary eyes hounded the Rankins. Johnny almost lost his breakfast when he glimpsed the leaded whips and rusty manacles that dangled from their saddles. He wondered if the men realized that their quarry was only helpless women and children.

The climb up Liberty Hill was somber. The front door stood ajar, mute testimony that the house had been searched yet again in the family's absence.

At the noon meal, Johnny noted his family's drawn faces. The strain of the dangerous secret was evident in all but the youngest children, who had not been told. Only Mother looked like herself—nettled.

"John, about your sermon." She slung mashed potatoes into a bowl and set the pot on the warming oven. "There was no need to be so blunt about the slave hunters. We all know what they are, but to say you would rather be caught robbing a hen roost is uncouth."

A spark gleamed in Father's eye. "Perhaps my remark was uncouth, but I meant what I said."

"Father?" Lucinda waited until she had his full attention. She shook her finger. "Have you been stealing hens?"

The entire family gaped at her before erupting into relieved laughter.

"Of course not, Cindy!" Johnny reassured his little sister. "You're big enough to know better than that. Can't you just see Father sneaking into Deacon Humphries's hen roost?" He tiptoed his fingers toward her plate while the smaller children giggled, but Cindy crossed her arms and glowered.

"You're right, Cindy," Father admitted. "Stealing hens is wrong. I'm sorry. Now be a good girl and help me bring in the platter."

She kissed his cheek and held the door open as Father bore a platter heaped high and golden-brown.

"Who wants some chicken?" Cindy asked with a prim smile. The whole family laughed again. "What's so funny?" she scowled.

Johnny's appetite surprised him. He helped himself to seconds on cold chicken and warmed over potatoes. Throughout the meal, he and the older children made a concentrated effort to keep the conversation light. As soon as the table was clear, however, Father crooked a finger at Johnny.

Once outside, Father took a careful look around. Right away he indicated the signal light that burned in the McCagues' window. Johnny offered a prayer of thanks that Eliza and her family were safe and started back to the house. To his surprise, Father caught his arm and led him to the shelter of his hedge apple tree.

"I've decided that you are to be conductor of this expedition, Johnny."

The shock was like cold water flung in his face. Johnny gulped. "Conductor?"

Father nodded. "It's your privilege to guide Eliza and her

family this time. She's your friend. I want you to escort her and the children to Arch Hopkins's place. Her daughter—well, I've heard her time is almost at hand. Bob Patton and Robert Poage will help with her, get her over fences and such."

"What about Sam? He knows Eliza, too."

"He would be missed as the sexton. You know you can't reach to light the candles for the evening service. No, you're the only one for this job."

The enormity of the task staggered him. Nine souls, counting the baby, and they were all his responsibility.

He calculated rapidly. Once Patton and Poage left Hopkins Hollow, their homeward journey would take them beyond Red Oak and most definitely away from Ripley. They would vanish like smoke and leave Johnny to walk home by himself long after nightfall while the woods teemed with slave hunters. He did not relish the prospect.

"May Hugh and Newt go with me?"

Father pondered his request. "That's a fine idea. You'll have to rustle them up yourself, though. Another thing. Take your pistol."

Johnny's heart plummeted to his boots. *As bad as that?* "All right. I'll have to get it from Aunt Esther."

"How's that?"

"Monty borrowed it." Johnny distinctly remembered that his cousin had orders to shoot a groundhog that had raided Aunt Esther's garden one time too many. If there was one woman in Ripley who was more feisty than Mother, it was her sister.

Father winced. "At this rate, everyone in town is going to be involved, but maybe it's for the best. This will be a challenge." He hooked his arm through Johnny's elbow to draw him closer. "Here's how we'll work it . . ."

Chapter 15

ELIZA

ELIZA SQUINTED AGAINST the sun's glare—noontime Saturday, near as she could figure. Her legs tingled with pins and needles, no matter which way she shifted. Summer locusts screeched from the deep shade. She wished she could stretch out under those trees and lie down.

She glanced at Beulah and the weary children—fast asleep. She stroked Beulah's head. Seemed like the other day she had dandled this daughter on her knee. *Lawsy mercy, where does the time go?*

A pile of corn shucks from the early morning feast lay at her feet. Eliza picked up a green shuck and fiddled with it idly. Could she make a doll with green shucks? She picked up three more green shucks; her fingers took over with practiced ease. Four shucks she laid together with the points at the bottom. She ripped a shred from another shuck; plenty to be had. A smile grew as she knotted the tops of the shucks together, pulled the tips over the knotted end, and tied off the head with another strip.

Her fingers flattened a husk and rolled it into a tube. She slipped it just below the head for arms and tied the ends off for hands. Then she tied the waist.

Time slipped away as she draped a shuck over the arms for shoulders and arranged more shucks for a skirt. She knotted them to the waist, and there it was, a girl doll for Mary. She squinted toward the sun—plenty of time to braid some corn silk hair.

Come nightfall, she had a pile of girl and boy corn husk dolls tucked away in Deacon Humphries's pockets. By then, the cool of the evening had seeped along the ground between the cornstalks and awakened the children. Eliza tussled to keep her grandbabies away from their mama; the longer Beulah slept, the better. Food in their bellies would do the trick, she decided.

Mary shucked corn and Shad kept the water dipper filled while Eliza parceled out supper. Every time one of the children fussed, Eliza promised a grand surprise to the one who kept the quietest. When even that diversion failed, she dreamed up another game.

"You children close your eyes," she whispered. "Whoever keeps them shut the longest will get the surprise."

Five little heads hit the quilt as Eliza swayed back and forth with Lulie. For a time, she saw furtive eye peeps, but eventually the children nodded off, Shad last of all. She laid Lulie down beside them and stretched to ease the crick in her neck.

Beulah snored once; Eliza shook her awake. While her daughter sought some privacy among the cornstalks, Eliza unwrapped the second quilt from the pile of household goods. She stuffed it with a few clothes and some corn shucks, tied it back together, and replaced it. When Beulah returned, she drank deep from the dipper Eliza offered, took a groggy look at her children, and fell asleep before her head touched the altered pack.

Eliza barely breathed. Sound asleep again, every last one of them. She groped through the pile of goods, picked up a few items, and headed for the branch. If a dog couldn't smell her when she walked in the water, she reasoned, it wouldn't scent all this plunder if she pitched it in the water, too. She knelt at the edge of the cornfield and slid the heavier objects into the water; whatever floated, she weighted with a rock. For the longest time she trekked back and forth until she was rid of it all. She reckoned she could trust the good Lord that no one would happen along this branch until time to harvest the corn.

She staggered back to her little flock, too tired to calculate how many hours she'd been awake now. Watch, Gil had said, and that's what she aimed to do. She stretched out on her back to watch the stars promenade across the sky until Sunday morning called them home.

When the sky read not long till dawn, she caught the stealthy tread of Gil's boots through the corn. God bless that man. She touched her vest, where the heavy pouch of gold was a comforting lump. The years of cooking and cleaning in Canada West—it was wonderful to feel the solid worth of her work, to know that she could buy her family's freedom with the sweat of her brow.

She sat up to the shock of Shad's eyes on her. The relief in his face—maybe he'd thought she was dead. She hugged him and held a finger to her lips. He nodded, and together they waited on Gil.

And then he parted the corn to one side and stared down at them. She read relief in his face, too.

"All right?" he whispered.

"Yessir." She handed Shad his shoes, stockings tucked deep inside and laces tied together. "Hang these around your neck. No use to put them on till we get all that caked mud offen your feet."

One by one, she awakened her sleepy grandbabies and draped their shoes over their necks. They gawked apprehensively at Gil; Eliza shooed him away. Then she slipped a hand into her pocket.

"You-all's been as good as gold. Mammaw's gonna give every last one of you a surprise." She handed Mary the corn husk doll with two braids. Eliza saw her eyes shine in the darkness. Quickly she distributed the other dolls. Joy banished fear, and Gil crept back.

Now she awakened Beulah, who moaned, clutched her belly, and immediately grabbed hold of her pack. She hefted it, realized it had lightened considerably, and opened her mouth to caterwaul.

Quicker than a blacksnake, Eliza clapped her hand over the scream. "Beulah May, look at me."

Beulah shot a sulky glare her way.

"See these children here? See that man? Well, quicker than a wink, we is all gonna be free, thanks to him. Free, Beulah." She looked at her grandbabies through eyes shiny with tears. "I saved us two quilts, a change of clothes, our shoes, and something to cover our heads. The good Lord will provide whatever else we need when we get to Canada West. Don't you dare scream." Beulah's head moved from side to side. "Soon, we is gonna be free." Eliza removed her hand and told Gil, "We's ready now."

But Gil did not move. There was a brightness in his countenance that she could not read. "Madame, across the river all are in great readiness to receive you. It has been my privilege to serve you. When I deliver you to Monsieur McCague's home, I shall bid you adieu." He bowed. "I am bound for Cleveland; I shall not see you again. But I wish to say that never have I encountered greater courage. And never have I encountered greater faith." He raised her roughened hand to his lips and brushed it with a kiss.

Eliza flustered; she drew out the pouch of gold. "Praise the good Lord for all you done for us. I pray a blessing on you all your days."

"Merci, Madame. And now, let us go." He swung chubby Georgie to his shoulders and struck out on the trail that Eliza had covered so many times that night. Deep joy lent wings to her feet until they arrived at the river. Under Shad's supervision, the children looked their fill at the vast expanse while Gil and Eliza helped Beulah over the side of Collins's skiff. Then Eliza whisked the children to the water one by one, like a mother cat transporting her kittens. Gil swung them over the side until all were stowed away. He pushed off and hopped athwart like thistledown. Two digs with the paddle, and they were on their way.

Georgie whimpered when the boat rocked in the current. Eliza patted his head and whispered, "Free!" in his ear. The word had a holy sound. She swallowed hard and tried not to think of Essie; by now the girl knew her whole family had up and left. Well, Eliza had trusted the Lord for so much. She asked Him to keep an eye on Essie, too. The water rippled from Gil's paddle into ever widening rings; it made her think of God's love spreading to encircle Essie.

In no time, the skiff bumped into Ohio land. Eliza was glad her feet were bare when she stepped on that hallowed ground. Her family was free.

The Frenchman's hands were a blur as he secured the skiff. He pressed Lulie into Shad's arms and pointed him up the steep bank to the McCague house. The boy scrambled like a sure-footed billy goat. The instant Gil saw Shad and Lulie disappear behind the lilac bush, Mary, Meesh, and Abe linked hands and scurried after him. Gil himself delivered cumbersome Georgie, and at last he and Eliza braced Beulah's back as she labored up the slope.

The street was narrow, but it seemed to Eliza that it took them an hour to coax Beulah across. The eastern sky brightened steadily until she despaired of ever reaching the fence. She rested her hand on her daughter's swollen belly as the muscles bunched. Sweat poured down Eliza's back by the time the trio ducked into the lilac bush.

Gil pushed a fence board that swung aside easily on a loose nail. Together they wedged Beulah through the opening like a too-big cork into a too-small jug. Gil held the board until Eliza squeezed into the McCagues' yard. Then she grasped the board and turned.

"God bless you, Gil," she whispered.

He was nowhere to be seen. The suddenness of his departure took her breath away.

"Come on, y'all get in the house," a woman urged. Her black bombazine dress rustled as Eliza trudged in her wake.

When Eliza entered the side door, the children were already out of sight. Ahead of her, a white-haired gentleman escorted Beulah to the stairs. He stopped on each step to accommodate her, but when she reached the first landing and glimpsed another flight of stairs, the poor girl sank to her knees and whimpered.

Eliza panicked. "Come on, Beulah, honey, we's gonna have us a bite to eat real soon. Wouldn't you like some spiced apple butter on a hot biscuit? Well, step along, and I'll give you some." Where the apple butter was coming from, Eliza had no idea, but Beulah licked her lips and mounted the step.

Shad's anxious face greeted them at the top of the stairs. His anxiety evaporated as he hugged his mother and Eliza and led them to a long, low-roofed attic room. Eliza wended her way past a ladder-back chair with a broken rung and a worn horsehair sofa as she dodged dried strings of apples. Best of all, she saw a rickety table which bore the makings of a feast.

"Guess what all they have for us to eat?" Shad hitched Lulie higher on his hip and tugged at his mother's sleeve. "Apple butter, Mama. Won't that taste good? And hot biscuits, too!"

"Well, you could just knock me over with a feather!" Eliza marveled. "Lookathere, Beulah May, just like I told you!"

But Beulah had already split open a biscuit so fresh that steam rose from the tender middle. She slopped on a spoonful of apple butter and rolled her eyes at the flavor. Eliza beamed; Shad's boyish laugh warmed her heart. He sounded like the cares of this world had rolled off his back.

The woman chuckled as she took Lulie from Shad. "That's

right, eat up! We have everything you need to make them comfortable, Eliza, but let them eat their fill, the poor lambs. Call me Aunt Kittie; everyone does."

Abe tugged at Eliza's skirts, a wedge of corn cake in his hand. "Mammaw?"

"What is it, honey?"

"This don't taste as good as my mama's corn cake," he confided as he licked golden crumbs from his fingers.

"Abednego! You say you're sorry!"

"Pshaw, no need." Aunt Kittie winked at Abe. "Your mammy must be quite a cook."

Peace and plenty. Eliza wanted to thank Aunt Kittie properly, but she rocked unsteadily on her feet.

"How long since you last slept?" Aunt Kittie's face swam in and out of focus as Eliza tried to prop her eyelids open. "Maisie!" she called. "Come take care of these children and their mama."

A firm grip on Eliza's elbow guided her to a bedstead. She sat down obediently and let Aunt Kittie fluff the pillow.

"Wake me up in a minute," Eliza murmured. "I gots to check on Beulah."

But it was a snore that disturbed her sleep. Eliza yawned and reached across to poke George—he snored something awful when he was getting a cold. A church bell's lovely tones swelled—Eliza counted seven chimes before she recalled that she was a long way from her husband. The snore must have been her own.

"Eliza!" The whisper had barely registered before the triangle door scraped along the floor and daylight flooded the tiny space. Aunt Kittie stood there. "My lands, I thought you'd never wake up."

"Sunday morning?" Eliza mumbled.

Aunt Kittie nodded. "I wish you could sleep some more, but Mr. McCague and I are on our way to church. I can't even spare

Maisie—we never miss the services. Keep those sweet lambs quiet while we are gone. And whatever you do, don't part the curtains along the riverfront, do you hear?" She pulled on her gloves. "When we get home, we'll know more about this evening." With that she was gone.

Eliza climbed out of bed and bumped her head on the low ceiling. She rubbed the knot and staggered into the large room, where the boys slid from the scrolled horsehair sofa to the floor with a thump. Georgie and Lulie clamored for their mama's attention; the instant Mary pulled one away, the other surged into the gap. Beulah ignored them all and kneaded the small of her back, her thoughts far away.

The best Eliza could say for her family was that they sported clean faces, hands, and feet. She asked a blessing on Maisie and took command.

"You children, hush!" Six pairs of eyes met the sternest gaze she could muster. "Lawsy mercy! We got to be even quieter than we was in the corn, you hear? Now you leave your mama alone." She glanced around the room. "Where's y'all's dolls that Mammaw made? Get them out so I can have me some of this good food Aunt Kittie left."

Scarcely had she collapsed on the sofa when a flutter caught her eye. Bright daylight flooded the room and filled Eliza with horror.

"Leave those curtains be, Georgie!" Eliza snatched him away, but not before she saw why Aunt Kittie had closed them. The river rolled right under the window. On the other side of the water, in Kentucky, mounted men and a pack of dogs searched the field where she and the children had spent a day and a night.

She backed away with her hand to her throat. "Keep him away from there, Shad," she choked out. Wordlessly the boy led Georgie away from the tempting curtains, but Eliza knew he had seen the same terrifying sight.

A horse whinnied on the street. The next instant a sharp rap echoed up both flights of stairs. Someone was at the door.

No, Lord. Eliza snatched the poker from the fireplace and hefted it. Beulah gathered the frightened children to her side, fierce as a mama bear. If they had been quiet before, they were still as death now.

Boot heels clattered in the hall downstairs. Eliza measured the distance between her and Beulah. Stay put, or position herself between her family and danger? She shifted her weight; the floor creaked. Then there was silence.

Did they hear that? She held her breath.

"Mammaw! I'm scared!"

Eliza was beside Meesh in a flash. She put a shaky finger to her lips, but it was too late. Hollow footsteps sounded on the stairs. Eliza whipped aside curtains at a back window and discovered an alcove where a lighted lantern burned. *If I can lower the children to the alley somehow . . .*

"Who's there?" A woman. "Mama Kittie, is that you? It's me and Mary! I thought we'd ride Raven over and go to church with you."

The door swung wide and the most beautiful lady Eliza had ever seen sailed into the room, red plaid skirts rippling in her wake. A baby girl clutched two handfuls of the lady's soft black curls. Her eyes were the blue-black of summer storm clouds, and they flashed fire.

"Oh, my word," she breathed. She disentangled the dimpled hands from her hair and faced the little girl away from her. The child stared at Eliza's family and gummed a finger as her mother said, "It's you. Those scoundrels across the river are hunting for you, aren't they?"

Eliza nodded mutely.

"Well, don't you fret. They shall never take you, not while there's breath in my body. I'm so sorry! We must have scared you half to death. Polly's peevish this morning"—she jiggled the girl—"cutting a tooth. We got a late start, but I thought my mare, Raven, would make up for lost time. Has Mama Kittie left you here?"

"She done left just a minute ago," Eliza said. "We'll be all right."

The lady's stormy eyes twinkled. "Yes, I can see that. Look here, you can put down the poker. I'm Mrs. Agnes Dickens Mc-Cague. Aunt Kittie is my mother-in-law and Polly's grandma."

The church bell tolled again, and Agnes sighed. "There—we are too late for church. May Polly and I stay here with you?" She indicated her daughter with a nod and a smile. "I don't think I could persuade her to leave, at any rate."

Then Eliza saw Mary, Lulie, and Georgie clustered around Agnes's daughter. Lulie inched a timid finger toward a silky black curl that peeped from Polly's bonnet. Polly spun on chubby legs and clumped across the floor in a plain invitation to chase her. Georgie squealed and waddled after her. Eliza grabbed him under the arms, but he stiffened and shot them straight into the air, a ploy which left no convenient handhold. He wriggled out of her grasp.

"Quiet, Georgie!" She flung the words after him and shook her head. "Lawsy mercy, he is a chunk to tote," she confided as she fixed herself a plate. "He can't walk so good yet, neither. He like to wore me and Shad out," Eliza sighed.

"Mama, it hurts," Beulah whimpered.

Eliza was at her side in an instant. "Beulah, honey, not yet. You gots to hold on." She helped her hobble to the green-striped sofa. "Now you just put your feet up and rest a spell." To her amazement, Beulah obeyed.

Eliza took a bite of ham and butter beans. "Like I was sayin', I don't know how we gonna manage him once we move on beyond Ripley."

Agnes hesitated. Outside, her horse whickered, and she broke into a broad smile. "Why, I believe I can fix that." Her speech quickened as she warmed to the idea. "I can put him in Polly's bonnet and clothes and hold him in front of me, and Raven can carry us wherever we need to go."

"Raven?"

Agnes strode to the window and twitched the curtains ever so slightly. A smile curved her lips and she beckoned to Eliza. She peeked out at the street below.

A coal black mare swung her hindquarters parallel to the hitching rack. She stretched her neck toward Kentucky, tossed her head, and bugled a challenge that rang over the water. When she pawed the dust, the flex of her muscles was beautiful to see.

Eliza stared at Agnes. "You'd take Georgie right through the streets among all those patrollers?"

"Why not?" Agnes demanded. "If we dress him up in her clothes, who will know the difference? People will think that I've taken my daughter out for a ride, just as I always do." She narrowed her eyes. "Say someone does become suspicious. I'd like to see the man who can take the baby off my lap to check." She laughed. "He'd have to catch Raven first, and when she sets her feet down, there's not a Kentucky nag that can overtake us." She waited for Eliza's decision.

There was a time when Eliza would have filed through the superstitions she set such store by, searching for some token to let her know what she should do. All at once, however, an image of Harriet Hopkins came to her, mounted and flying across Hopkins Hollow with the wind in her hair.

Eliza faced Agnes. "Bless your heart," she said. "Take him."

Chapter 16

JOHNNY

JOHNNY APPROACHED TARBELL'S tavern. He studiously avoided the rough crowd gathered there, but he could not help hearing the announcement.

"That's right, boys! Five hundred dollars goes to the man who delivers the fugitives to me." A raspy chuckle punctuated the offer.

Laban Biggerman.

Johnny crossed the street. From the corner of his eye, he watched the slave trader gurgle from a jug and wipe sweat from his brow before adjusting his hat on a pelt as red as a fox's. His evil eyes glowed yellow. "Yessir, a man works up a powerful thirst huntin', don't he? Hey, there, young feller, come on over here and have a swig," he heckled Johnny.

Hearty guffaws greeted the invitation. Johnny fought panic and forced himself to ignore the man as he strolled to his Aunt Esther Carey's porch.

Esther opened the door at his knock, took one look at his face, and yanked him inside. "Just what do you think you're doing, sashaying around Ripley while that man is here?" she scolded.

He rubbed his arm where she'd grabbed a hold. "Father says I need my pistol, but I loaned it to Monty. May I have it back, please?"

Aunt Esther tapped a foot and cupped a hand to her mouth. "Montgomer-y!"

"Yes, ma'am?" His cousin's answer was tentative.

"Johnny's here for his pistol. See that you load it for him," she commanded.

"Yes, ma'am."

She rounded on Johnny. "I plugged that infernal groundhog at last. I swear, he purt near ate us out of house and home." She rapped on the wall. "Montgomer—oh, here you are." Monty cringed as his mother snatched the gun and thrust it at Johnny.

"Thanks, Aunt Esther."

But she gripped his arm. "Now, Johnny," she said, "you boys think you know all about guns, but I can teach you a thing or two, if you'll listen." She gave his arm a shake. "Say you get out there in the dark woods all by yourself, and you see somebody out looking for that poor woman. Now, what will you do if he gives you any sass? I'll tell you what you *don't* do. Don't you aim that gun at his head; he'll dodge, and you'll miss." She slit her eyes. "No, sir, you aim for his white shirt front. You'll see that easy enough in the dark, and one shot will go straight to his heart." She nodded with satisfaction.

Johnny gulped. "All right, Aunt Esther, I'll do that." He started to hug her but thought better of it.

The stern lines of her face relaxed. "God go with you, son," she caroled. "See you at the evenin' service. Bye, now." She chivied him out the door like dust under her broom.

He ducked down the back alley and cut across lots toward the church. The sun dipped toward the Kentucky hills and a twilight haze gathered. Tavern bells chimed early candlelight time on each street. Biggerman had roused excitement until the normally quiet town was in an uproar—most everyone wanted that five hundred dollars. Father would be livid; he always harped that the tavern-keepers' licenses hinged on keeping an orderly establishment.

In a matter of moments, Johnny reached Bob Poage's back fence across the alley from the church. He hoisted himself up on a hitching post just outside the gate. As the tavern bells faded, he pulled down his hat brim and positioned himself so he could view the side yards of several houses in a row, clear to Front Street.

The time for evening service drew near. Conversation buzzed as folks gathered on their doorsteps to set off for church. Johnny hooked his ankles around the back of the wooden post to keep his legs still. He retrieved the dried peach stone from his pocket and hollowed out the center with his Barlow knife while he waited.

From somewhere in town, he heard a horse stepping it off at a pretty good clip. *Biggerman?* Johnny tucked his chin almost to his chest and listened. Mulberry Street, that's where the horse was. He risked a peek, ready to signal an alarm if he glimpsed the chestnut gelding Biggerman favored.

But it was a black comet that skirted the corner and snorted fire. Mrs. Agnes McCague spurred Raven west along the alley, her daughter perched on a knee.

"Howdy, Johnny. Going to church?" She flashed past as little Mary crowed with delight.

No time to reply; they were already out of easy earshot. Johnny gawked in open-mouthed admiration. *She scared the living daylights out of me, but my goodness, is she ever a beauty!* Married or not, the sight of Agnes lifted his heart.

He smiled, eased his awkward posture a particle—and met Mary Ann Hay's scalding glare. *Oh, no!* Johnny's ears were hotter than fire by the time she broke eye contact and flounced into the church between her parents.

He was so flustered over her snub that he almost missed the first refugee. A trio emerged from the lot beside him. The first person was Bob Patton—no mistaking his bulk, but for once his laugh was missing. He supported the arm of a lady whose

face was concealed by her bonnet; Robert Poage had hold of her
other arm. To the casual observer, she looked like a rheumatism-
hunched old woman on her way to church, but Johnny had been
around enough birthings to observe that Beulah's time must be
very near. The three inched past the church and vanished into
the brush at the foot of the hillside.

One. Count six children plus Eliza and Beulah and then
light off up the hill like Biggerman was on their tail, Father had
said. The problem was sorting the runaways from the Ripley
residents on their way to church. He knew everyone in town,
but he would have to look sharp to spot them once Sam rang
the church bell.

He stretched and threw a glance over his shoulder. Hugh and
Newt stood at the back door with Mrs. Poage. He wished he
could be with them as they joshed each other, but that was not
behavior befitting a conductor.

The vesper call rang out, and the street bustled to life. In the
midst of a passel of church ladies, Johnny spied Eliza. She carried a baby. *Two. Three.*

His eyes itched, but he dared not rub them. So many people
passed back and forth across the street at once that he was afraid
he might miss a crucial one.

Here came a little boy he'd never seen. He scampered to the
Evanses' door. Now a bigger boy entered the Poage house. *Four,
five.* Another one, a girl this time. *Six.* A boy skipped into the
Evanses' house; *seven.* Now a few more men crossed. The street
cleared.

Johnny's heart thudded. What had happened to the eighth
fugitive? Before he could think, his charges poured through
the fence. Two boys the same size tugged like kites at their big
brother's hands. An older girl hitched up her skirts like a lady
as she stepped through the opening. Newt rushed to the fence
to help Eliza and the smaller girl through.

Johnny counted noses and added Beulah. *Seven.* He broke out in a sweat. *What now?*

He jumped about three feet when somebody whacked his arm.

"What are we waiting for? She said seven's all." Hugh pointed.

Then Johnny saw Eliza grin so wide that the gap in her teeth showed. She bobbed her head yes. If he'd had time, he would have hugged her.

His legs trembled as they set out. Six freed slaves and three scared white boys crossed the alley and stole behind the church through the friendly dusk. Brush crackled as Johnny shoved it aside at the foot of the hill. Newt took the smaller girl from Eliza for the duration of the steep place, and they climbed the stone steps to the red house on the hill.

The door stood open. Father waited there, hat on head and walking stick in hand. Mother tied her bonnet strings; her eyes glistened.

"God bless you, Eliza," she said as she looked at the family. "Together at last."

Eliza wore a smile so proud she looked like she'd bust wide open. She touched each child's head in turn as Johnny shifted uneasily, one eye on town.

"Shad, Mary, Abe, Meesh, and this least one's Lulie," she told Mother as she took her from Newt. "Thank you for all you done for us."

The two women embraced and Father shook Eliza's hand. "If you follow orders, you will be safe in Canada before you know it. God go with you, Eliza. Come, Jean, we mustn't be late for the service." He paused. "Take good care of them, son," he told Johnny. He crooked his elbow at Mother and escorted her down the hill.

Never in his life had Johnny missed his family like right

now, when they were all at church, and he faced this greatest danger alone. He plucked up his courage and trailed behind the others.

"There's the fireplace where me and your Uncle Mose dripped all over the place after I crossed the river on the ice," he heard Eliza tell her grandchildren. Newt herded them past the kitchen toward the back door where Hugh waited.

There was a scuffle. "Come back here," Newt exclaimed. "Stop them, Johnny!"

Johnny barred the door as the twin boys tried to dart around him. "Where do you think you're going?" he asked the twins.

"Me and Abe left our hats out front. We gots to get them before we go." One boy said it, and the other, as like him as his own reflection, nodded.

Nervous laughter bubbled up and Johnny had a hard time holding it back. "Well, that's good manners, but you can't show your faces out there anymore." He fished around the corner for the hats and the boys' faces lit up when he handed them over. "Now march." He flashed Hugh a tired grin.

Eliza squeezed his arm as they all flocked together on the porch; the gesture was oddly comforting. Johnny closed the back door and tested it to make sure it was unlocked.

"You go first," he ordered Hugh. "See if anyone's watching."

Hugh's eyebrows shot up, but he nodded. He scouted both corners of the porch before he struck out for the potato patch. He halted at the edge, scanned the semidarkness, and motioned with his hand for them to come ahead.

Lulie dived at Newt even before he reached to take her back from Eliza. She latched on to his hair with both fists. His eyes widened in alarm; Johnny and Hugh suppressed snickers and led the way.

When they had crossed the second cornfield and reached neighbor Tom Smith's wheat field, a surprise awaited them.

"Mama!" Shad spotted her first. He hung back from the two big men who supported her.

Eliza was at his side in an instant. "It's all right, Shad. These men are going to help your Mama walk."

He measured them up, nodded, and stuck tighter than a burr to his mother's side.

Johnny peered at the field that lay before them. Even in the rapidly fading light, it was easy to see that Tom Smith had plowed this field, and recently, too.

"Oh, my," Hugh breathed. "What if he has a piece left to plow?"

The way to plow a field was to start at the outside edge and guide the horses in an ever-diminishing circle. If the plow rested in unbroken ground close to the center . . . Johnny fingered the carved peach stone in his pocket and signaled to let down the fence. No help for it; their path lay across this field to the gate that let out on a road only a quarter of a mile from Hopkins Hollow.

It took forever for the men to assist Beulah across the lower bars and onto the loose soil. Eliza made good use of the time, Johnny noted. She had all those grandchildren except Lulie shoeless and sockless, with knotted laces draped around their necks before he signaled them to cross the fence.

Soon he wished he'd removed his own boots. The children's bare toes navigated the fine topsoil with ease. After he'd slipped for the umpteenth time and tried to shake loose crumbs of earth down to the toe of his boot, his heart soared with admiration for capable Eliza.

And then, by the light of the rising moon, he caught a glimpse of the plow. The story in the earth was plain. When the farmer and his hired men resumed work tomorrow morning, eleven sets of tracks would greet them.

The grave men, his crestfallen friends, and a serene Eliza—all looked to Johnny for guidance. He knew they had not a moment to lose. Truth to tell, he wasn't certain they would make it to Hopkins Hollow before Beulah's time came. The desperate rattle of her breathing goaded him to hurry. Yet, they could not hurry; every step pained her. His only comfort was in knowing that Tom Smith and his family had often aided fugitives. "Push on," he ordered.

The fresh breeze wafted the sharp scent of weeds under a wavery, orange moon. Johnny and his friends opened the gate at last. Tall grass and Queen Anne's lace grew undisturbed on the path that wound down the hollow to the Hopkins place. Mary tried to press a bouquet into her mother's hands. Eliza took it instead and tucked the white flowers into her kerchief. Her comical expression as she preened for Mary made even Johnny smile.

In front of the Hopkins's house, Johnny saw the huckster's wagon that would convey Eliza and her family to the next safe house. The younger boys were all for sprinting ahead to explore it, but Johnny kept a tight rein on their antics. He marveled at their burst of energy. His own shoulders stooped like he was about a hundred years old.

Father's idea for a conveyance was nothing less than inspired. Huckster wagons—who gave them a second thought? They were as common as water. All summer long, the hucksters traveled from farm to farm with goods to tempt the lady of the house. The ladies traded homegrown produce for the wares, and the hucksters traveled on to Cincinnati to sell the fresh produce in the city.

Johnny had to admit that he shared the younger boys' enthusiasm for the wagon. It was a two-horse hitch with open sides. Wherever the huckster stopped, he dug out a weight with a ring at the end. He hitched his horses to that, and he was in business. The open sides served as a storefront. The novelty for Johnny was the canvas sides that unrolled to block off the interior from prying eyes.

Before Mr. Hopkins limped out to join them with a lantern, Johnny and the boys took a good look inside. At the end of a long day, the wagon should have been laden with produce, but instead, a bed of straw invited weary bodies to stretch out. The back gate had been removed, and somebody had dragged an upping block to the opening. Eliza's grandchildren jigged with delight when they realized that they were the fortunate ones who got to ride in the huckster's wagon. All but Lulie swarmed up the step and bounced in the deep straw with muted squeals.

Mrs. Hopkins crossed the clearing with stately grace, a finely dressed baby in her arms. Johnny rubbed his eyes. *Why, that's little Mary McCague.* He recognized her bonnet. *What's she doing here?*

Baby Mary reached for Eliza with a crow of delight. Johnny started. He had heard that very cry earlier when Agnes galloped Raven past him in the alley.

And then he knew. The eighth fugitive! Tears of relief stung his eyelids as he watched Eliza gather her grandson in her arms, the little dress ridiculously out of place now that Johnny knew the secret. Agnes must have brought this boy straight up here all those hours ago. No wonder she had practically laughed aloud as she smuggled a fugitive right under his nose; it was a brilliant plan.

"Don't lollygag around, now." Archie's querulous command spurred Johnny into action.

Eliza crossed the yard. "How you doin', Old Archie?"

He scowled. "Don't you 'Old Archie' me, woman." Johnny heard Eliza's delighted chuckle.

"Sit tight in there!" Johnny ordered the children. "We have to get your mama into the wagon now.

Bob Patton and Robert Poage steadied Beulah at the back

of the wagon. Her face was gray and her arms trembled as they assisted her up the steps and walked right in beside her. She collapsed in the straw.

"This baby's comin', Mama." The plaintive words were no more than a whisper.

Johnny had never seen two women move as fast as Eliza and Mrs. Hopkins did when they sprang into the wagon.

"Take these children across the yard and tell Harriet to bring baby things right away," Mrs. Hopkins directed, and Johnny was glad to temporarily give up command.

He glanced at his friends. Hugh's jaw dropped and Newt looked green around the gills. Clearly this was more of an adventure than they'd expected. Both of them ignored the wagon and did their best to amuse Lulie and Georgie while the older children played hide-and-seek.

Minutes later, they heard a whimper and a cry. Harriet Hopkins emerged from the back of the wagon, her face wreathed with smiles. "A healthy girl," she announced with pride.

Johnny checked the older children's reactions. A new baby was nice, but nothing out of the ordinary—he certainly knew the feeling. Their expressions said the next leg of the journey could not start fast enough.

In a little while, Eliza poked her head out and motioned to Johnny. "I want you to see her," she said.

Johnny left his friends in charge of the children. He gazed at the tiny red-faced baby, all swaddled up in her grandma's arms. She was very quiet, and that was good; she had a long way to go in secret.

All at once, he knew this baby was different. From the moment of her birth here in Ohio, she had something that her grandmother had toiled for all her life—freedom.

His throat tightened and he winked back sudden tears. "She's beautiful."

"I gots a good name for this here baby," she told him. Her laugh rang out like a bell. "You tell your mama and papa we named her Glory!"

Johnny nodded, but he could not smile back. "You're going away now."

Eliza steadied him with her words. "You done been like a son to me, Johnny. All the time when my family was so far away, you talked to me and helped me. I will never forget you." She grasped his chin and kissed his forehead.

"I wish I could see you again sometime, so I know if you got to Canada West all right."

Eliza beamed. "We'll get there, by and by. And you'll see old Eliza again," she said firmly. "You'll see me with the good Lord in glory, Johnny, and won't we have us a time when you get up there? What a day that will be!"

He wiped away tears as she retreated to the shadows.

Too soon, Harriet and Mrs. Hopkins rejoined Arch, their aprons splotched where they'd wiped their hands. The children left off chasing fireflies and clambered into the wagon again. Hugh groaned as he swung Georgie aboard. Johnny unhooked Lulie's hands from Newt's hair. She puckered up to cry until she saw her grandma's welcoming arms.

Eliza's grandchildren stared solemnly at Johnny from the back of the wagon; Shad in particular locked eyes with him until the huckster replaced the gate and unrolled the canvas at the back. Just before the man tied down the last strap, several hands waved frantically. Then the huckster flirted the traces and whistled to his horses. The wagon lumbered into the darkness with its precious cargo of nine souls, bound for freedom.

"Lord love them," Mrs. Hopkins sighed. "You boys want to spend the night?"

"No, thank you, ma'am. We're expected at home." Johnny squared his shoulders. "Let's go, boys."

"She was a great lady," Archie mumbled. He recovered and brandished the lantern. "Skedaddle, now."

The Red Oak Creek bottoms appealed to Johnny for the last leg of the journey. Tired though the boys were, speed seemed like a mighty good idea. Hugh and Newt soberly followed Johnny's lead. It had been a long night.

When the boys reached the edge of Father's woodlot, Johnny heaved a sigh of relief. He fidgeted while Hugh took a breather. "Come on!" he urged. He turned around and almost ran smack into Zeke Means.

It was impossible to tell who was more startled, but Johnny recovered his poise first. He fingered the butt of his pistol. "What are you doing on our property?"

Means hefted his rifle and sighted along the barrel. "Coon huntin'."

He reeked of whiskey. Means stared fixedly at Johnny, Hugh, and Newt in turn. He pondered three against one thoroughly, tipped his hat, and slunk toward the road.

Johnny motioned with his hand to hold everyone steady until Means was out of sight. Then the boys flew across the woodlot with a turn of speed worthy of Raven. They collapsed against the house and gasped for breath.

To Johnny's surprise, Father opened the door. "Praise the Lord," he said with great emotion.

Mother hovered behind him, her face gentle. "Welcome home, boys." She led them up the stairs to the empty bed that Johnny usually shared with Sam and Andy. "They are spending the night in town," Mother explained. "Turn in and get some sleep. It's a pity you'll have to go to school in just a few hours, but it can't be helped." She laid her hand on Johnny's arm. "You did a fine thing tonight, son. Sleep well." She adjusted the signal lamp in the window, smiled again at Johnny, and left the room.

The next morning at school, Johnny was surprised to find that he didn't feel tired at all. He glanced across the aisle at Newt; no ill effects there, either. His gaze wandered to Mary Ann at precisely the moment she looked at him. Pleased, he colored up and fastened his eyes on Hugh, who was manfully reciting his history lesson.

His mind wandered a bit as he listened—he'd forgotten to tell Mother about the baby. *A new little citizen.* His mouth turned up at the corners.

He gave himself a mental shake. Maybe he was pretty tired after all, if he couldn't keep his emotions in check any better than that.

Recess was better. Every big boy in the school joined in a rousing game of crack the whip. Johnny's legs pumped to keep up with the line, but he tumbled and rolled when the fellows snapped him. He scrambled to his feet and whooped. Wonderful to be just a boy again.

At the end of the day, Hugh and Newt had not so much as winked at him about last night's adventures. *True friends, that's what they are.*

The school day weathered safely, he climbed the hill for home. *These old steps*, he thought. *How many have climbed this way to freedom?* He yawned widely and pushed open the front door.

"Hello, Johnny. Look who got home last night!" And there was Lowry, right beside Mandy.

Something about his big brother had changed, he noticed right away. It wasn't a beard. Lowry stuck to the conventions of the old days, just like Father, and remained clean-shaven. No, Lowry's eyes held secrets of some sort. What had happened while he'd been away?

He soon found out. Lowry had been offered a church in Illinois. The whole family opined about it over supper. Johnny flung an accusing glance at Mandy. He'd told her long ago that she would leave someday, and now his words had come to pass.

He could not stay angry at her, though, and he joined in the excited planning for the move.

Then Sam burst into the room.

"Have you heard what's going on in town?" He was breathing hard.

Fear clutched at Johnny's heart. *Has Eliza been captured?*

"Tell us, Sam." The color had drained from Father's face.

"Tom Smith's hired men found footprints, a whole lot of footprints, when they went out to finish plowing his wheat field. They wanted to claim the five hundred dollars. Tom told them both that they would have to walk to town if they wanted to do that. Then he fired them when they did."

Every eye swung to Johnny. He fished the carved peach stone from his pocket and rubbed it between his finger and thumb until the smoothed surface squeaked.

"Don't worry, son." Father shook his head. "They can't prove whose footprints those are, and there is no chance they will find out."

"Wait, Father," Sam said. "All that happened this morning. Laban Biggerman himself went up to inspect the field this afternoon. He swears those are the slaves' footprints. And that's not all." Sam got to the meat of his news. "Just below the fence that lets out on the road to Arch Hopkins's house, Biggerman found a little red stocking. He said he'd know it anywhere; he was half crazy, waving it around. Tom Smith and Hayden Thompson just laughed at him. But Biggerman was right, wasn't he?"

"What do you think, Johnny?" Father waited.

Johnny retraced his steps frantically. *How in the world could anyone lose a stocking out of a shoe?* And then he knew the answer. The children had carried their shoes and stockings while they walked across the freshly plowed ground. Perhaps one of the boys had dropped it and noticed the loss, but decided not to retrieve it after the ruckus over their caps.

He nodded shamefacedly at Father. "Yes, we could have lost it. What now?"

Father considered for a moment. "Smith and Thompson have already done us a good turn by making fun of Biggerman's find. We'll just have to take a chance and let the story die down. They'll search all day anyway. But no one will think to bother Arch Hopkins. They'd never believe he had anything to do with Eliza, so most likely their search will take them far past his place. But Johnny," he continued, "I can't take a chance with you."

Johnny hung his head. All these years later, his storytelling still followed him like his shadow. "I'm sorry, Father."

Father shook his head. "You don't understand, son. We can't take a chance that the lost stocking will lead back to *you*."

He remembered his loneliness when Mother and Father left for church, just last evening. It was nothing to the great gulf of emptiness inside him now, when the full weight of his responsibility threatened to crush him.

"I believe I know a way out."

It was Lowry who spoke. Johnny raised his head without much hope.

"I'm going to be working hard to start the new church in Illinois," his big brother said slowly. "Mandy and I will need help, and we don't know a soul out there." All of a sudden, Lowry radiated confidence. "How about sending Johnny along with us?" His smile warmed Johnny's heart.

Mandy chimed in, her blue eyes starry. "Oh, Johnny!"

Johnny looked at Father for guidance. *Would it be enough?*

"It does seem like the good Lord has made a way for you, son, if you will go." Father's relief was visible. "Out of sight, out of mind. But it's your decision."

Mother, Father, and his brothers and sisters all watched as Johnny tried to make sense out of the rapid turn of events. He thought of the Stowes and all the family members they had lost, and of Eliza's long struggle to reunite her family. How could he leave his own family now that he finally understood what they meant to him?

At the back of his mind, Eliza's words echoed: *You been like a son to me.* Maybe she had the answer, after all. Maybe Lowry and Mandy needed him to be part of their family now, just as he had been part of Eliza's when she had no one.

Still, Illinois is a long way from Ripley . . . and Mary Ann Hay, he realized. He stared into the distance as he thought about her amber eyes, always watching. "Mayn't I ever come back home?"

"Why, of course you will come back!" Mother reassured him. "Just let this blow over for a while; that's the idea."

"All right." He heaved a sigh. "When do we go?"

"First thing in the morning. Thank you." Lowry clapped his shoulder. It was hard to believe Johnny had ever looked on him as an adversary.

Dawn found Johnny binding up his trunk. He did not have much to pack, after all. The one snag in the hasty plan was that Lowry, as a preacher, was chronically short of funds. By the time he'd paid the captain for two tickets, he had only a nickel left over. The Lord provided again—the captain offered to let Johnny wait on tables and wash dishes to pay his fare. Whatever was left over he would share with Lowry and Mandy.

Newfound appreciation for his family made his good-byes tender. Before he left, he wandered to the shelter of his hedge apple tree with Cutie at his heels. He stared at the Kentucky shore. Had it been only two mornings ago when he feared for Eliza's life? *How much has happened since then!* Most importantly, his friend was reunited with her family, and they were free.

He patted Cutie's head. "Bye, girl." The old dog's tail thumped. She curled up with a sigh in the early morning shade.

The change that loomed before him was huge, but it had all the trappings of a fine adventure with his new family. *And the sooner we start, the sooner I'll be back.* He took the stone steps two and three at a time, his trunk balanced on his shoulder.

When he reached the riverboat, he stowed his trunk and summoned Lowry. "I'll be right back. Don't leave without me!" he joked. Lowry shook his head, draped an arm around Mandy, and waved as Johnny tore down the gangplank.

Right, left, and left again he sped down the alleys and streets of Ripley like Laban Biggerman was on his trail. He dodged wagons to cross Third Street.

"Watch out there!"

The rusty voice stopped him short. A red-gold gelding danced backward as the rider reined him in. The horse's head drooped. Sweat caked its scarred flanks; pink foam dripped from a cut mouth.

Johnny gulped. His eyes were level with dusty trousers. Manacles jingled from the saddle; the rider himself towered above him. Slowly Johnny took in the shirt and vest drenched with sour-smelling sweat, the hard line of the mouth, and the sun-bleached red mustache. Bloodshot eyes bespoke a long night with whiskey for company.

Biggerman.

The slave hunter squinted down at Johnny against the early morning sunlight. "What's your hurry, boy?"

For a moment, Johnny forgot how to breathe. "Sorry." He dodged aside.

"Hold on." The man wiped his mustache with the back of his hand and stared hard at Johnny. "You know where them Rankins live?"

Does he suspect? "Everyone knows that," Johnny answered truthfully.

Biggerman glanced at the house on the hill and shrugged. "Reckon so." He squinted at Johnny again. "Them Rankin boys, now, they all look alike, don't they?"

"That's what people say." *So far, so good.* His hand trembled ever so slightly as he gripped the peach stone and waited.

The weary gelding shifted its weight. Biggerman yanked at the tender mouth. "Stand still!" He blocked the sun's rays with an upraised hand. "The one they call Johnny—you seen him recently?"

Johnny considered. "Not face to face." Every nerve in his body thrilled with the impulse to flee.

"But you seen him someplace." Biggerman smiled, sure of himself. "Any idea where he is right now?"

"I really can't say." Johnny shook his head with regret.

The smile faded from the man's face. He sneered. "Well, you're a worthless young pup, ain't you? Guess I'll have to hunt down Johnny Rankin myself." He raked the jaded horse's flanks with his spurs, and they disappeared in a choking swirl of dust.

Dizzy with relief, Johnny squeezed his eyes shut until the morning bustle of business claimed his attention. Ladies in bright dresses sallied forth with market baskets hooked over their arms, men gathered at the horse trough to swap news, and children scuffled through the dust for the sheer joy of raising a cloud. *Oh, how good to be surrounded by friends!*

He left Third Street behind. Soon he came in sight of a porch full of white and blue morning glories that fluttered against a thick curtain of heart-shaped leaves. He checked the sun. *Pretty early to go calling.* He knocked on the door.

"I'll see who it is, Mother." Mary Ann Hay shouldered the door open, both hands full of thick strands of copper hair to be braided. A sky-blue ribbon trailed from her fingertips.

"Oh!" Her wide, amber eyes stared at Johnny, first soft with surprise, then with an unmistakable glint. She pursed her lips. "If you're looking for Agnes McCague, you have the wrong house."

Ouch. "Mary Ann, I'm sorry. She startled me when I had something else on my mind."

Mary Ann finished one braid and started on the other without a word. He had a crazy feeling that he would like to help her do up all that red hair.

He tried again. "I don't blame you for being miffed with me. I wish I had more time to make it up to you, but something's come up pretty sudden." He scuffed at the porch with the toe of his boot. "I'm going to Illinois with Lowry. He and Mandy need me; he's starting a new church there."

She stepped outside. "Illinois?" It sounded impossibly far away, the way she said it. Her eyes welled. "When are you leaving?"

A blast of the riverboat's whistle startled them both. He knew she read the answer in his eyes. "I wanted to know if you would write to me while I'm gone."

"I will," she answered shakily.

Funny how those two words made his heart glad. "I have something for you." He fumbled in his pocket. "I carved it out of a peach stone from our orchard." He opened his hand to offer a miniature basket.

She gasped. Golden lights danced in her eyes. "For *me*, Johnny? Thank you!" She examined it with delight. "Why, it's no bigger than the end of my thumb!"

The smooth sides reflected the early morning light. "I was going to give it to you anyway, but now you can keep it to remember me by until I come back."

She clasped it to her cheek. "But I don't have anything to give you!"

"Give me your hair ribbon, so I can recall how pretty your hair is." He tugged gently at the end of her coppery braid.

She blushed pinker than a wild rose and slipped a ribbon into his hand. He put it in his pocket.

"Mary Ann, who are you talking to?"

The question interrupted a long look that passed between

the two of them. This time Johnny did the kissing. He backed away slowly.

"Good-bye," he breathed. "Remember, you promised to write!"

Her pink lips trembled ever so slightly as she nodded. "I-I wish I could go, too. I'll miss you so."

Johnny smiled. "Oh, I'll come back someday. And when I do, nothing in this world will ever part us again."

Mary Ann's eyes grew as big as saucers. Behind her, the door opened. Mrs. Hay tiptoed to peer around her daughter.

"Johnny Rankin! What are you coming to see my Mary Ann about, so early in the morning?"

Mary Ann spread her hands in a silent apology.

Johnny winked. "It's a secret."

Historical Note

WHEN JOHNNY RANKIN met a slave woman just after she crossed the icy Ohio River with her baby in 1838, he had no way of knowing he was witnessing history. In fact, years later he wrote that there was nothing special about the woman called Eliza.

Who was Eliza? Some records say her real name was Mary and one source refers to her as "a woman named Armstrong," but there is no doubt that she was a real person. Several Rankin family members recorded bits of Eliza's story many years after her adventures. Johnny's brother Cal (Richard Calvin Rankin) wrote that two different slave women escaped across the ice at nearly the same time. Another brother, Sam (the Reverend Samuel Gardner Wilson Rankin), was the source for an 1895 newspaper account about Eliza's escape, her husband's escape, and how Eliza returned for her daughter and grandchildren. Johnny's father, the Reverend John Rankin, wrote in his autobiography that Eliza was "redeemed by the blood of the Lamb."

During his long life, Johnny recorded several versions of Eliza's story in great detail. Johnny, Mother, Father, Ibby, Cal, and David were the only eyewitnesses when Eliza passed through their home the first time. Since Johnny was an eyewitness who told the story so many times in his later years, I chose to make him a main character.

The Rankins told family friend Harriet Beecher Stowe the story of Eliza some time after the escape. Stowe honored her promise to keep the Rankins' involvement a secret, but she made no such promise about Eliza. By 1851, the world read Eliza's story in the *National Era*, a famous anti-slavery journal which serialized *Uncle Tom's Cabin.* Johnny began to sense Eliza's unique place in history. After all, he had met and helped Eliza, who was now immortalized in a chapter called "The Mother's Struggle."

It is difficult to overstate the influence of *Uncle Tom's Cabin.* Mrs. Stowe's novel portrayed slaves not as dumb beasts of burden, but as men, women, and children created in God's image. She showed that even though some slaves were treated better than others, their fortunes could change for the worse in the twinkling of an eye because they were seen as property, not people. Mrs. Stowe did not hold back as she described beloved family members sold away from each other at an owner's whim, or slaves beaten senseless over a trifling offense. As a result, "*Uncle Tom's Cabin* contributed to the outbreak of [the Civil] war because it brought the evils of slavery to the attention of Americans more vividly than any other book had done before."[1]

Little wonder that Johnny was anxious to share his part of the story, as scripted by God. But as is so often the case in real life, there was not a neat storybook ending to his youthful desire to tell Eliza's story. By the time "The Mother's Struggle" tugged at America's heartstrings, Johnny was twenty-five years old; he and his wife, Mary Ann, had two children. The Fugitive Slave Law, enacted in 1850, required the American government to actively assist owners in recovering their runaway slaves. Now more than ever, the Underground Railroad, its passengers, and its conductors must remain a secret.

Uncle Tom's Cabin became an instant best-seller when it was published in book form in 1852; 300,000 copies sold that year. The story was presented on the stage from the 1850s to the 1910s.

---

1. Harriet Beecher Stowe House, "*Uncle Tom's Cabin*, Slavery, and the Civil War," Harriet Beecher Stowe's Life & Time, www.harrietbeecher stowecenter.org/life/

Before Johnny died in 1914, a silent movie version of the story was filmed. The character of Eliza was well-known in America during Johnny's life. (I had forgotten until recently that one of Maud Hart Lovelace's Betsy-Tacy books includes several chapters in which Betsy and her friends earnestly desired to see the stage version of *Uncle Tom's Cabin* when it came to Deep Valley in 1904.)

The part of Johnny's story that fascinated me was the active role played by the strong women he knew. Johnny was a bit like Luke, the beloved physician of the Bible. He wrote more about the women of Ripley and Red Oak than did the other Rankin men, just as Luke wrote more about the women involved with Jesus' earthly ministry than did the other Gospel writers. Aunt Kittie McCague, Agnes Dickens McCague, Aunt Esther Carey, and Johnny's mother, Jean, were full partners with their husbands in the dangerous work of the Underground. Likewise, Harriet Beecher Stowe ably attended to her duties as a wife and mother, but she also moved a nation with her vivid account of slavery's cruelty.

Eliza herself was the equal of anyone she met, wise, and brave. Once I began writing this book, it became clear that Johnny would share the main character spotlight with Eliza. I am convinced that he would have wanted it that way. I am pleased to share the rest of Johnny's and Eliza's story, the rescue that Johnny recorded with such care as he reached the end of his life.

It's important to note that Laban Biggerman is a composite character and the names of the slaveholders have been changed. The rest of the people really lived in southern Ohio during the time this story takes place. For some, like Dr. Greenleaf Norton and Mary Ann Hay, I had not much more than a name to go on. For others, like Archie Hopkins and Jolly Bob Patton, Johnny included more detail. He wrote perhaps thirty pages total, but his descriptions are full of life.

The sieges, the visit to Lane Seminary and Johnny's friendship with the Beechers, the lost red stocking, Agnes McCague's ride, Gil's story (although his real name is unknown), and too many other incidents to name really happened. As for Eliza, according to tradition she eventually returned to free the granddaughter left behind, the girl I called Essie.

Of course I didn't get every detail right. I greatly anticipate the day when I will join the Rankins and Eliza in glory. I can almost feel the Lord's good pleasure when He introduces us all to each other. What a day of rejoicing that will be!

For more information on Harriet Beecher Stowe and *Uncle Tom's Cabin*, visit:

Harriet Beecher Stowe's Life & Time at www.harrietbeecher stowecenter.org/life/

The Library of Congress: American Memory, Today in History, June 5 at www.memory.loc.gov/ammem/today/jun05.html

1910 Vitagraph Film of *Uncle Tom's Cabin* at www.iath.virginia .edu/utc/onstage/films/mv10hp1.html

FIELD TRIPS

The National Underground Railroad Bicycle Route passes through Ripley: www.adventurecycling.org/routes/ undergroundrailroad.cfm

National Underground Railroad Freedom Center in Cincinnati, Ohio: www.freedomcenter.org/

Rankin House, Ripley, Ohio: www.ohiohistory.org/places/ rankin/

FOR FURTHER READING

Lovelace, Maud Hart. *Betsy and Tacy Go Downtown*. New York: Harper Collins, 1943.

Stowe, Harriet Beecher. *Uncle Tom's Cabin, or Life Among the Lowly*. New York: Aladdin Classics, 2002.

The Rankin Family Legacy

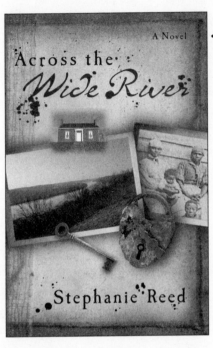

A Novel

Across the Wide River begins the inspiring story of the Rankin family. Lowry Rankin knows that slavery is wrong. Ever since he was young he's helped runaway slaves travel farther north to freedom. But he's grown tired of trying so hard to fix a problem that won't go away and brings him nothing but trouble . . . so now he's on the run. Will Lowry stop running from slavery—and God's call—and take a courageous stand for freedom?

"*This novel captures the excitement of the period, its dangers and moral dilemmas. There is romance and adventure. And, essential to the traditions of the Rankin family, there is witness to the role of God in mankind's affairs, both great and small.*"

—JAMES B. POWERS
Rankin family descendant

"Across the Wide River *plunges young readers into the life and death drama of the pre-Civil War Underground Railroad.*"

—PETER MARSHALL
Author, *The Light and the Glory* and *From Sea to Shining Sea*

Kregel
Publications